I0743460

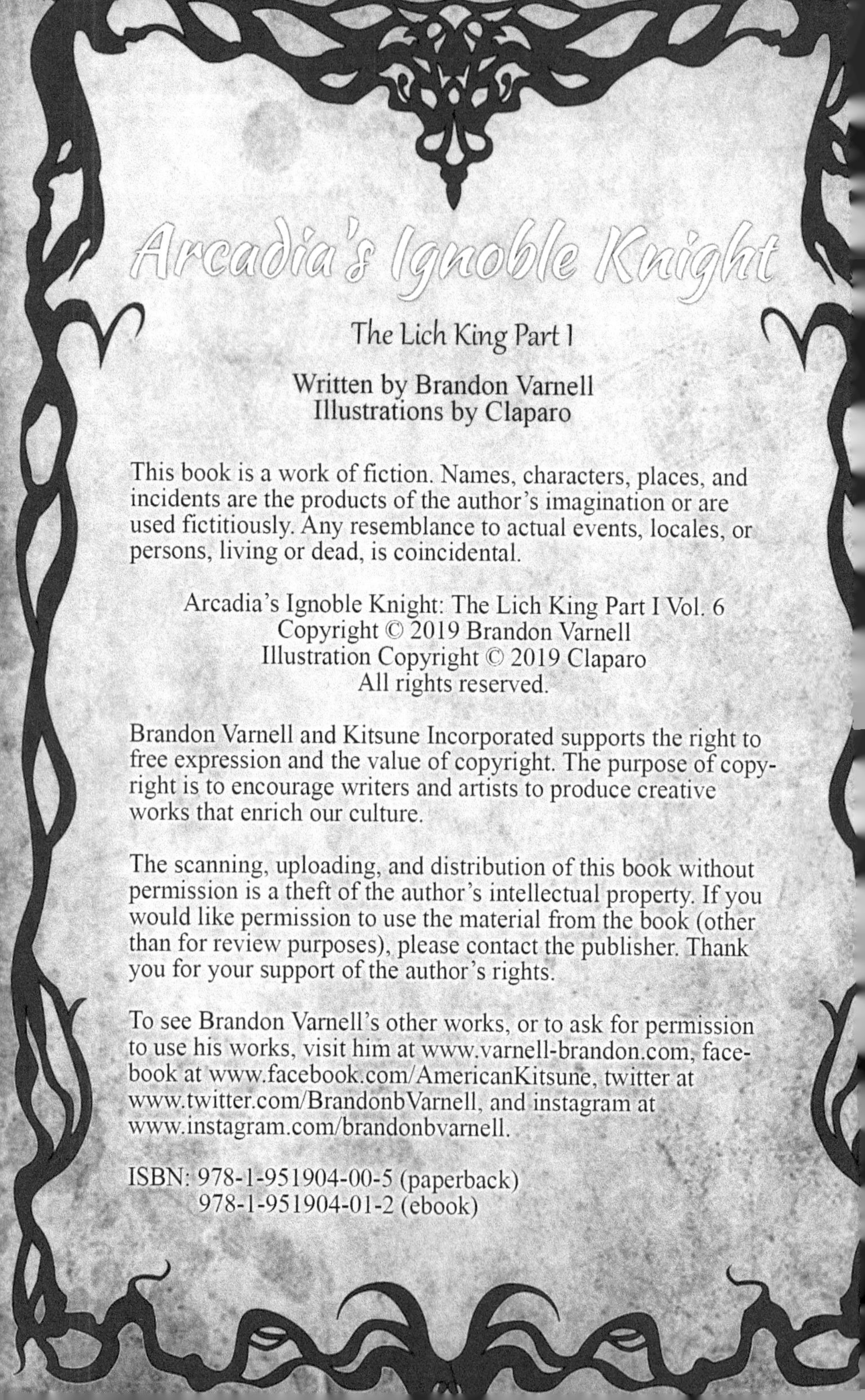

Arcadia's Ignoble Knight

The Lich King Part 1

Written by Brandon Varnell
Illustrations by Claparo

This book is a work of fiction. Names, characters, places, and incidents are the products of the author's imagination or are used fictitiously. Any resemblance to actual events, locales, or persons, living or dead, is coincidental.

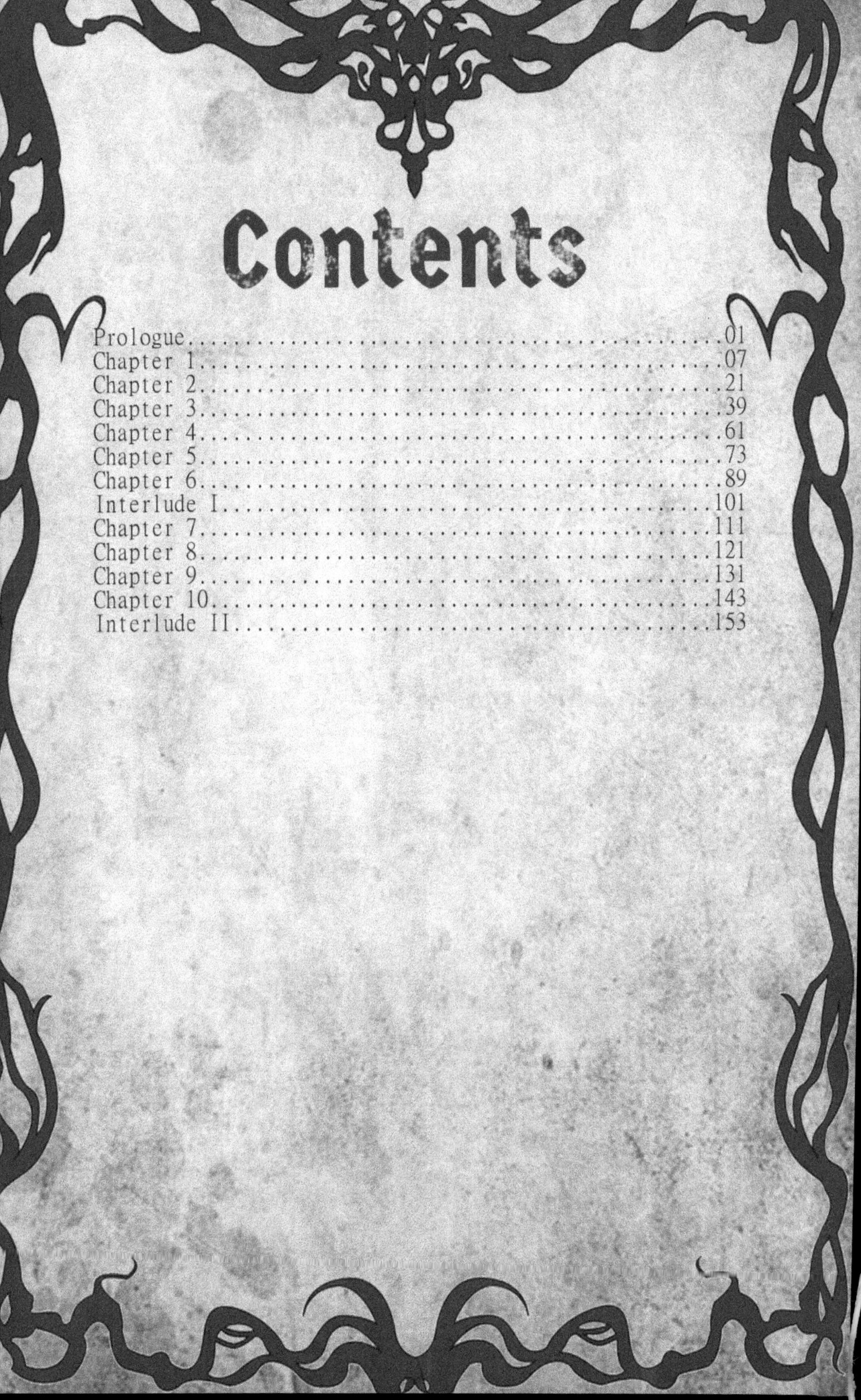

Contents

The story so far...

Elincia has been outed as an elf and all of Cassadinia is now aware of her origins. To help her avoid being discriminated against and perhaps even persecuted, Sylvia sends Caspian and Elincia on a journey that will take them far from Arcadia's capital...

Prologue

Caspian and Elincia stood in Sylvia's office, in front of the lady herself, who sat behind her desk, a stern frown marring her face. Raven locks of hair framed her delicate features. Her silver eyes gazed upon them with a coolness that was reminiscent of ice. Her body, clad in a dress that was simple yet somehow seemed imposing, barely shifted as she sat with her hands clasped in front of her body.

As always, the oldest living sorceress was composed. Her expression gave nothing away. In all the time that Caspian had known her, he didn't think he had ever seen her smile, not once.

Behind Sylvia stood D'artagnan, her knight, the man currently known as the strongest knight. Glistening armor shone from the sunlight piercing through the window behind him. His hand rested lightly on the hilt of the sword sheathed at his waist, as though he was ready to draw it at any time. He, like his sorceress, retained a calm composure. Caspian thought it made him look like a statue.

"We are currently facing something of a crisis," Sylvia said, and, much like her face, her collected voice gave none of her emotions away. She really did remind him of ice. "News that you are an elf has spread, and it has been causing much unrest among the people. They are frightened."

It had been about a week since the incident with Davidson, since people had discovered that Elincia was an elf. It hadn't been so bad at first. Many people hadn't treated her any differently, but the further the rumor spread, the number of people who began showing fear toward her increased. Last time they went out, a majority of the people they walked past had whispered horrible things about her, and a few people had even thrown stuff at her and told her to go back to Fas Sheras. Just remembering what happened during those times made Caspian angry.

Only a few people still treated Elincia like a human being. Mr. and Mrs. Légumes didn't treat her any differently. They, along with many other people who worked or shopped at that particular open market, had said that it didn't matter if she was an elf.

While he and Elincia were grateful for their support, they didn't want to get those people involved in their conflict. Neither of them would be able to forgive themselves if something happened to the few individuals who still treated her kindly. That was why they had stopped going for their morning walks through that market.

"I'm sorry," Elincia said quietly, her shoulders slumping.

Caspian reached over and discreetly held her hand. His emotions flared through their bond. He tried to shower her with the love and affection he felt for her through their connection, which caused Elincia to straighten and her cheeks to flush red. She cast him a grateful smile, and her hands tightened around his. Right now, this was all he could do to support her.

Sylvia looked down at their hands and frowned. Thankfully, she didn't say anything.

"I am not blaming this situation on you," she said at last. "In truth, the fault lies with me. I should not have kept this secret for so long."

Astonishment coursed through Caspian like a bolt of lightning.

Had he ever heard Sylvia admit to being wrong? No. Never. Granted, he had rarely interacted with her on his own, but still, the times they had interacted when he was younger, she had never once admitted that she was at fault.

"W-what? Lady Sylvia?" Elincia looked even more surprised than him, a consequence of her living with Sylvia for most of her life, no doubt.

When Elincia had been rescued after the rebellion at Fas Sheras, the last remaining elven kingdom, Sylvia had brought her to this very mansion. Here, in this place, Elincia had lived. While Caspian, who had also been rescued by Sylvia, had gone on to Arcadia's Knight Academy, Elincia had never once lived elsewhere. One could almost say that she was a bird locked away in a cage.

She knew Sylvia even better than he did. That must have been why she expressed even more surprise than him.

"My original plan called for you building up a reputation of good will first," Sylvia explained. "My hope was that the people would see you for who you are, rather than what you are. I wanted them to become taken in with all of your good qualities. I wanted them to respect you for your accomplishments and compassion, so that when we finally announced that you are an elf, they wouldn't care because they know who you were as a person first."

In theory, Caspian thought that Sylvia's plan was sound. If people spent enough time with someone, had the chance to judge them without prejudice, then when they suddenly learned a huge and potentially damning secret, it wouldn't have mattered. They wouldn't have cared because their perception of that person would have already been cemented. That was the theory anyway.

However, theory and practical application were two different things. Caspian wasn't sure if Sylvia's plan would have worked even if this incident hadn't happened. Then again, he would admit that he didn't have much faith in humanity's ability to accept people who were different.

"Now that this has happened, what should we do?" Caspian asked. "Ele can't do her job if no one will even speak with her. Even worse, the situation might escalate if she goes out. Suspicion and distrust will follow her, and it will only increase as time goes on."

"Please address Elincia by her proper title, Caspian," Sylvia admonished him. Behind her, D'artagnan shuffled his feet. "Since Elincia's presence is currently a cause for concern, we have decided to send you on a task that will take you out of Casadinia and return after the situation has settled. This task will likely take several weeks, maybe even a month, depending on how difficult it proves to be."

Caspian glanced at Sylvia's knight. D'artagnan el Melloi was a middle-aged man with angular features. His face appeared to have been chiseled from stone, further hardened by his intense demeanor. Long bangs framed his face, and a light fringe hovered over eyes of burnished steel.

He wore light armor. His leather jerkin rustled whenever he shifted, dark brown and freshly polished. The shoulder pauldrons, greaves, and vambraces that he'd donned were made of steel, and they shone brightly underneath the light of the afternoon sun, which streamed in through a window at his back.

That reproving look he's giving me...

Caspian wondered if D'artagnan also felt the irony at Sylvia's statement. How many times had her knight told him the same thing each day, that he should address the sorceresses by their proper titles, or that he should call them Lady Sorceress or some such? More times than he could count.

"You're sending me away?" Elincia asked.

Caspian winced. That tone, suffused with such sadness, caused a sharp pain to pierce his chest. It made him want to hold her and never let go. The only reason he didn't pull her into his arms right then was because Sylvia would have disapproved.

He had no desire to be lectured.

"Just temporarily," Sylvia assured her. "Given the current climate, having you here isn't a good idea."

"You mean that my presence might incite riots," Elincia said, her voice making it clear that she was on the verge of tears.

"Yes," Sylvia admitted. "At the moment, your presence is

causing a lot of problems. Just as Caspian said, you can't do your job as a sorceress if the people you're duty bound to protect don't even accept you."

Elincia stifled a sob, and Caspian, not knowing what to do but wanting to do something, stepped closer and placed his hand on the small of her back. It was a small thing, but he hoped it would help.

"It'll be okay."

"Caspian?"

"Everything will be okay. We'll get through this."

"What's our task?" asked Caspian out loud.

"Your task will be to investigate the rumors of a necromancer appearing in the north-east part of the Ruudon Province," Sylvia continued, either not seeing or, more likely, willfully ignoring the physical intimacy between him and Elincia. "We've received several reports of the dead rising from their graves and attacking the living. Caspian, I believe this task will be of personal interest to you."

Caspian felt a chill run down his spine. It wasn't just what Sylvia had said about their new task being of personal interest to him. A necromancer was a major threat. Caspian knew that from personal experience.

"Why do you say that?" asked Caspian.

Sylvia graced him with a grim look. "Because there was a rumor among the reports that the necromancer has taken residence in Parumé."

6

Chapter 1

Parumé… how long had it been since he had heard that name? Not since his rescue at Sylvia's hands, he wagered. It was almost surprising how he could remember that name, but then, given his history with it, perhaps he should have realized that he wouldn't be able to forget his past so easily.

Caspian looked at his luggage, which, to be honest, wasn't much; he had a spare set of clothes, several pairs of underwear, his knives, his sword and sheath, and some toiletries like his toothbrush and soap. He didn't need much. Even if they were going to be away for a couple of weeks, it wasn't like he that many necessities to bring along.

It was still morning. He and Elincia had left Sylvia's office to get ready for their trip. They would be taking the train to Axium, and then they would take a carriage to Parumé, which had no train tracks running through it. Axium was the furthest out the trains ran in that direction.

"Caspian?" The door opened and Elincia walked in. "Are you ready?"

"Yes." Caspian finished putting his clothing inside of his bag. After slinging his sheathed sword around his shoulders, tucking his knives into his boots, and then grabbing his bag, he turned to face Elincia. "I'm ready. How about you?"

"Um, I've got my luggage ready," she said in a timid voice.

Because they would be traveling incognito, Elincia was wearing a long brown traveler's cloak. It covered her entire body all the way down to her ankles. The cloak came with a hood. It wasn't pulled up right now, but once they left the mansion, it would go up to hide her face from the citizens. While they might be a bit conspicuous, it was better than the alternative.

They didn't want anyone discovering who she was once they left, for obvious reasons.

"Then let's go and get your luggage," Caspian said as he walked to the door that she had entered his room from. It was the side door that led into Elincia's room.

"Ah, w-wait!"

Elincia grabbed his hand, stopping him in his tracks. Caspian turned around and looked at her. The emotions spilling out from between their bond were a jumbled mess, so he couldn't make heads or tails of them, but that hardly mattered. Her expression told him enough.

"Is something wrong?"

After a moment of hesitation, Elincia let go of his hand and took a step back. "N-no… it's nothing."

If Elincia thought she could lie to him, then she must have forgotten about how well he knew her. Still, now wasn't the time to call her out on it. They needed to get ready.

"Come on," he said, taking her hand and pulling her into her room.

Elincia wasn't finished packing. Her clothing lay haphazardly on the bed, a mess of different colored shirts, dresses, and socks. It looked like she was going to take five times as many outfits as him.

"I'll help you get packed," Caspian said without complaint as he walked over to the bed. He grabbed the first pair of clothing he could find. He was going to just fold it up and put it in the suitcase that sat on the ground by the bed.

He paused.

Holding up the article of clothing in his hands, he realized that there was surprisingly little fabric. The garment in his hands was pink and lacy and didn't look like it would cover much.

"Ah…" He blinked. "This is…"

"Noooo!!" Elincia rushed forward, grabbed the racy undergarment, and yanked it out of his hands before cradling it in her arms as though trying to hide it from his eyes. Her own eyes had embarrassed tears leaking from them. "P-please don't look at them! My heart isn't prepared for you to see them yet!"

As the startling realization that Caspian had been holding a pair of Elincia's underwear in his hands set in, heat sprang to his face like a bonfire. He tried to speak. He couldn't. His throat had closed up as his embarrassment reached critical mass.

"Uh… ah… ah…" Caspian choked for several seconds as he struggled to respond. Then… "Ah… I'm sorry."

The pout that Elincia wore, complete with dark red blush spreading across her cheeks, was adorable, but he was too busy dealing with his own issues.

"I can't believe you grabbed my underwear. Out of all the clothing you could have grabbed first, why Caspian? Why did it have to be my undergarments?"

Caspian turned his head. "I didn't mean to… sorry."

"I can't believe this," Elincia whined, looking like nothing could embarrass her more than she was now.

The ensuing awkward silence was nearly deafening. Caspian couldn't even look at Elincia as she stood back up and walked over to the bed. His face felt hot enough to fry an egg.

She placed her underwear in her bag, and, without saying a thing to him, began to put her clothing into her suitcase. Caspian watched her for a second out of the corner of his eye. Gulping, he came to a decision and decided to help her. He didn't say anything. He just walked up to her left side and started folding her clothes alongside her.

Neither of them spoke another word as they worked. Caspian couldn't think of anything to say, and knowing her as he did, Elincia was probably too embarrassed to say anything at all. Despite that, the two of them finished folding Elincia's clothing in record time.

"Done," Caspian said. He grabbed her suitcase and lifted it with a grunt of effort.

"It's not too heavy, is it?" Elincia asked.

"Naw, it's fine." Caspian hefted the suitcase over his shoulder. "I've got this."

Leaving the room, Elincia and Caspian walked through Sylvia's mansion, toward the entrance. Sebastian Forde should be outside the front entrance with the MAFT ready. They didn't want to keep him waiting too long.

"Master Caspian! Mistress Elincia!" a shout reached them before they had walked too far.

Turning, they were greeted by Cassidy charging toward them, tears in her doe-like brown eyes and cheeks flushed with what he guessed was sorrow.

Cassidy was their maid. Their personal maid. Technically, she was Caspian's personal maid, but since he and Elincia were a pair, she attended to them both.

Her curly brown hair bounced as she ran toward them, and the ruffled hem of her maid outfit fluttered about her feet clad in heeled shoes. She was jogging quite quickly. Caspian's danger senses were going haywire.

"Master! Mistress! What's this I hear about you leaving?! Surely you can't be—waaaa!"

Cassidy's innate clumsiness came into play when she tripped over her own two feet. With all the grace of a drunken ballroom dancer, Cassidy fell face first to the ground. Her body skidded across the polished marble for several meters. She stopped in front of Elincia and Caspian, her face planted into the marble, and her butt sticking high in the air.

"Ow…"

"Are you okay?" Elincia asked as Caspian knelt down and helped the poor woman to her feet.

"Is it true?" Cassidy ignored the question and asked, tears in her eyes and nose red. "Is it true that you two are leaving Casadinia?"

"Just temporarily," Caspian said. "We'll probably be gone for a few weeks, but we'll come back before too long."

"Why didn't you tell me?" Cassidy asked.

"We just found out ourselves," Elincia said. "We haven't had a chance to tell anyone yet."

"But how am I supposed to get ready if I don't even know we're leaving?"

Caspian and Elincia glanced at each other. It sounded like Cassidy was under the assumption that she would be coming with them. However…

"I'm sorry," Elincia said gently. "But, you can't come with us."

Eyes bulging as though they might fall out of their sockets, Cassidy stared between them with an expression of bafflement. "I-I can't—why not?"

"Because where we're going might be dangerous." Caspian scratched the back of his head. "Our task might involve eliminating a necromancer. You know what those are, right? Necromancer's are undead monsters, a coagulation of tormented souls that have manifested into a single, malicious entity. They're incredibly dangerous."

Cassidy was a maid. She had no fighting capabilities. They couldn't take her on such a dangerous task. Neither of them wanted to see their friend get hurt, or worse, killed. Caspian didn't think he would be able to live with himself if something like that happened to this girl.

"But I—" Cassidy sniffled "—I want to be with you two."

Caspian didn't know what he should do in this situation. Fortunately, Elincia wasn't clueless like him. She pulled Cassidy into a hug, which the maid didn't hesitate to return. Caspian looked away.

He felt awkward looking at them, like he was seeing something that he shouldn't, though he had no idea why he felt this way.

"I'm sorry. I would love it if you could come with us." Elincia sighed as she ran her hands through Cassidy's long hair. "But we can't take you. It will be much too dangerous. I'd never forgive myself if something happened to you."

"I understand," Cassidy murmured. Her voice was muffled, which Caspian realized was because she had buried her face into Elincia's chest. He looked away again. "I understand why I can't come with you two. I just wish I could."

Caspian waited patiently until the two were done hugging. He scuffed his foot along the floor, trying hard not to look at them. If he did, he would become embarrassed, and he didn't want that.

Elincia sniffled a little as she and Cassidy pulled back. There were tears in her eyes now as well, though none of them fell as she looked at the maid who had become her good friend.

It seems there's been a lot of teary-eyed moments this morning.

This was probably just as hard for Elincia as it was for Cassidy; the two of them had bonded a lot in the past six months. They often spoke with each other, took baths together, and stayed up all night giggling over erotic novels—which Caspian had unfortunately discovered one morning when they forgot to hide a volume of *The Master and the Maid* when he'd come into Elincia's room to wake them up. Elincia and Cassidy were almost like sisters now. At least, that was how it appeared to him.

"Don't worry," Elincia said. "We won't be gone for too long. We'll be back in a few weeks. Hopefully, things will have settled down by then."

"Right." Cassidy wiped the tears from her eyes, straightened herself out, and then smiled at them both. "Master Caspian. Mistress Elincia. Please have a safe journey."

"We will," Caspian said as Elincia nodded.

"There you are!" a voice suddenly shouted. "Slacking off again, are you?"

Cassidy froze solid, like a block of ice. Her body shuddered in fear. She turned, slowly, as though she was afraid of what she would find waiting for her.

A squeak escaped her as Lacy, the head maid and a woman who no one dared mess with in this mansion, marched down the hall.

Her blonde hair was tied into a severe bun. The headdress she wore was bigger than Cassidy's, as if declaring that she was more important than Erica's former maid. A black and white dress with numerous frills adorned her outfit. Unlike Cassidy's modest cut, this woman's maid uniform had a significant dip in her front, which exposed a good deal of cleavage.

"I thought I told you to clean the bath houses!" Lacy grabbed Cassidy by the ear, eliciting a loud yelp from the younger maid, and pulled the girl down the hall. "Come on! I'm going to work you to the bone! Consider this your punishment for not working when I told you to."

"No! I'm sorry! I promise I'll clean the bath houses! Please! Nooooooo!!!!!!!"

Caspian and Elincia remained silent as Cassidy was dragged around a corner. They would have said something had she been dragged off by anyone else, truly, but Lacy terrified the both of them. Their maid's kicking feet as she struggled to escape Lacy's ironclad grip were the last things they saw of her.

"I think we should head out now," Caspian said quietly.

Elincia nodded. "I agree."

***

Walking through the train station, Caspian and Elincia did their best to remain inconspicuous. They moved through the throngs of people, men and women and children, who sometimes traveled in large families and other times were alone. A pair of businessmen walked in the opposite direction as them. Four people, a mother, father, and their two daughters, walked hand in hand several meters away so as not to get separated. There were all kinds of people present.

A large, vaulted ceiling towered over their heads. Massive

columns several times taller than any human jutted from the ground, connecting to the ceiling and acting as support. Many people strolled between these columns. They made their way onto and off various platforms, where steam engines and trains came and went.

Caspian had already bought their tickets at the station outside, so he and Elincia didn't need to worry about being stopped. He held her hand as they traveled through the mass of people. His excuse had been that he didn't want them getting separated, but really, he just wanted to hold her hand.

The train they hopped on was a standard steam engine. Gleaming steel shone brightly in the overhead lights. Smoke rose from the smoke stack up front, black plumes that ascended into the air, floated up to the ceiling, and filtered out through several vents that had been opened for just that purpose.

Because their tickets had come out of Sylvia's pockets, they were granted the luxury suite. Just like the one that Erica had used during the time when Caspian had temporarily protected her in Derek's place, this one was an expression of opulence. Their feet sank into the red carpet. A large bed sat on the left most corner of the room, and a window situated about a meter to the bed's right allowed natural sunlight to filter in. This suite also had a couch, a table, and a bar with various alcoholic beverages.

Caspian could only shake his head at the extravagance. It was so unnecessary.

"This room is so big," Elincia said. "It's nothing like the compartment I was in when I traveled to Axium."

"You didn't get a luxury suite?" Caspian asked as he closed and locked the door.

Elincia shook her head as she traveled further into the room with soft, delicate footsteps. "I had to use my own savings to get those tickets, since I had snuck out of the mansion to get there."

Her words caused a wry smile to tug his cheeks. "I'd love to say that the idea of you sneaking out of the mansion is unheard of, but I know you better than that."

Wandering over to the bed, Caspian set down all of their

luggage, unstrapped his sheath, and placed his sword against the wall. He glanced at Elincia. She had already taken off her cloak and kicked off her sandals. Now dressed in a simple green gown, she sat on the bed, leaned back, hands supporting her from behind, and kicked her feet in the air. Her cute little toes wiggled as she moved.

"Check out this bed, Caspian," Elincia said with faux cheer. "It's so soft!"

With a wan smile, Caspian sat down on the bed. His body sank next to Elincia's. He then placed a hand over hers.

"Maybe now we should talk about whatever's bothering you."

Elincia froze. "Y-you knew?"

"Who do you think you're talking to?" Caspian asked, grinning. The grin left as he moved his hand, lacing his fingers through hers. "I'm your knight, Ele. I'm always watching you, so I know when something is bothering you. Even if I couldn't tell that something is wrong from your expression, I still get a sense of what you're feeling through our bond."

Knights and sorceresses went through a bonding ceremony that tethered their lives together. It was originally an elven marriage ceremony, but Sylvia had it modified for humans. According to her, the ceremony didn't do much aside from let knights and sorceresses know where their partner was.

For Caspian, a half-elf, and Elincia, a pureblood elf, the Knighting Ceremony meant far more than it did for a normal knight and sorceress pair.

Their lives had become inextricably linked, their fates eternally bound together, their souls tethered by threads of magic that exceeded the standard bond of sorceress and knight. Through the bond, they could get a general idea of the other person's emotions. When they were in physical contact, they could even speak to each other through telepathy.

The bond was still growing. Caspian was sure that once it solidified, they would be able to speak telepathically even over long distances and even hear the other's thoughts and feelings.

Her shoulders slumping, Elincia sighed. "I guess there's no

point in hiding anything from you, is there?"

"Probably not," Caspian agreed. He bumped his shoulder against hers. "So, what's wrong?"

"Parumé," she said. "The look on your face when Lady Sylvia mentioned that we were going there seemed almost frightened. It was like you were scared after hearing that name."

"Ah."

Caspian should have known that she would have noticed his fear. Just like she couldn't hide anything from him, he clearly couldn't hide anything from her. They'd known each other too long. The bond also went both ways. It wasn't a one-way road.

Looking at the ceiling, Caspian studied the designs that were painted over it, swirling golden paint against a crimson backdrop. It really was too luxurious. He wished they had gotten a normal compartment.

"Parumé is… my hometown." He sighed. "It's where I lived before Sylvia saved me. I lived there with my mom for the five or six years of my life. About… eleven or maybe twelve years ago, the village was destroyed. I remember coming home one day after hiding in the forest. The village was on fire and everyone had been killed."

"Oh, no…" Elincia held a hand to her mouth. "Then… your mother?"

Caspian closed his eyes as if doing so could block out the memory. "Everyone. The entire village was gone, slaughtered, but it wasn't a regular attack. It was no bandit raid or anything like that." He paused. "The people were killed by undead."

Undead. The name was self-explanatory. They were human corpses that had been brought back to life through necromancy. It was a cursed magic no living creature could accomplish. Only necromancers and liches could bring the dead back to life.

"I remember only a bit about my past," Caspian whispered in a hoarse voice. "Most of my memories feel as if they have been blotted out. I can no longer recall them. Out of all the memories I do have, this one remains the most vivid. I remember how the dead had overrun the village, indiscriminately killing everyone there. The screams as people were torn apart remains as clear now as it did back then, as though it has been seared into my eyes. I remember… my mother, she used magic to protect me, even as the undead ripped her body apart."

Caspian placed a hand over his face and squeezed as though trying to force the memory out of his mind. It had been a long time since he thought about that day. Now that he was thinking about it again, images came to him, blotting out his vision in sprays of carmine fluids.

During the first few years after his rescue, Caspian had been constantly haunted by nightmares of that day. While the nightmares had all but vanished, that didn't mean the memories had disappeared. They were still there. They lurked in the darkest corners of his mind, waiting to spring forth and torment him again.

"It's so strange," Caspian spoke with a soft, hesitant voice. "I remember exactly what happened that day so vividly, but even now, I still can't recall my mother's face."

Whenever he tried to imagine his mom, her face always came to him as a black spot, as though the memory of what she looked like had been purged from his mind. The few times he had tried to recall what she looked like, his head would ache. It was like his own brain was telling him not to remember.

Perhaps I am better off not remembering.

"Oh, Caspian," Elincia murmured with a voice that sounded like she might shed tears at any second.

Because his eyes were closed, Caspian was surprised when he felt a body gently lean into him. He fell onto the bed. It was so soft that his body sunk instead of bounced. Opening his eyes and looking down, he stared at Elincia, who lay on top of him.

"I'm sorry for asking you to dredge up such terrible memories," she said.

Caspian wrapped his arms around Elincia's waist, so supple and thin that she seemed to fit perfectly in his arms, as though she had been made to be hugged by him, or his arms had been created for the sole purpose of hugging her. The warmth from her body was a greater panacea than anything else he could think of.

The bond between them was alive at their contact. Through it, he could feel her regret and also her love. Despite the heavy topic, her feelings, which seeped into him like water being soaked into a sponge, made him smile.

"You don't need to apologize. I would have told you about this at some point, even if our destination wasn't Parumé. You deserve— no, I want you to know everything about me."

Elincia pushed herself up. Straddling his waist, she placed her arms on either side of his head, resting on her forearms, their faces barely a centimeter apart. She was so close that Caspian could feel her nose touching his. Her eyes, brilliant in ways that not even aquamarine could have hoped to match, stared at him with a gaze filled with so much love it stole his breath away.

"You know that if there's anything I can do for you, all you need to do is ask, right Caspian?" she said, whispering.

"I know," he said, also whispering. He reached up and placed a hand on the back of Elincia's head. "And I can think of at least one thing that you can do right now."

Elincia's cheeks were pink. No doubt she could feel what he wanted through their bond. It wasn't like he could mask his desire for her.

Through their bond, he could also tell that she desired the same thing he did.

The smile that broke out on her face was like a ray of pure sunshine.

"That's not something you need to ask me to do. It's… it's what I want to do."

"Is that so?" Caspian murmured as he threaded his fingers through her soft, golden tresses.

"It is so," Elincia responded by lowering her head even further.

With only a bit of effort, Caspian guided Elincia's lips to his.

The world around them disappeared.

Chapter 2

It took six days to reach Axium. The distance between Casadinia and Axium was approximately 16,053 kilometers. A train could normally travel that far in less than two days, but that was only if it never stopped. There were dozens of stops along the way.

Since there wasn't much to do on the train, Caspian and Elincia spent most of that time either talking or lounging around. They also spent a lot of time kissing. In fact, Caspian was almost certain they had spent more time kissing than anything else, save maybe speaking to each other through their bond, which had become a habit by this point.

Their bond was strengthening, or so Caspian believed. They still needed physical contact to speak telepathically. That much hadn't changed. However, their ability to sense each other was getting stronger. Now Caspian could tell exactly where Elincia was within a 150-meter radius. It wasn't just accurate either. He could also sense her emotions from that distance, too. Her thoughts remained indistinct, elusive, but her emotions, provided they were not overwhelmingly muddled, were as clear as day to him. He could tell when she was sad, happy, frustrated, or confused.

Since this was a two-way bond, Elincia could feel his emotions as well.

The two of them were snuggling on the couch when the train slowed to a stop. Caspian glanced out the window and saw that they were inside of the station. He sighed.

"It looks like this is our stop," he said.

"So it would seem…"

Elincia seemed reluctant to get up, but she climbed off his lap anyway. Caspian stood up and went over to their luggage. He strapped his sheathe over his shoulder, slung his tote back across his back, and grabbed Elincia's suitcase.

"Loki?" Elincia called out.

Caspian felt a surge of mana fill the air. He glanced at her ears and watched as the pointed tips vanished. Right before his eyes, her ears seemed to grow shorter and become rounded just like a human.

"I've got everything," he said.

"Hm. Thank you for carrying my luggage."

Elincia smiled at him, which caused his insides to grow warm.

They left the compartment and traveled down the hall alongside the other passengers who were leaving. Caspian took the first step outside. He turned around and offered his hand to Elincia, who placed her hand in his and allowed him to help her down.

"I know it's only been six months, but it feels like I haven't been to Axium in forever."

"I think I understand how you feel. The tournament feels like it happened such a long time ago."

Now standing on one of several train platforms, Caspian and Elincia looked at the train station of Axium. It seemed so much smaller than he remembered. Of course, that may have been due to how used to Casadinia's massive size he had become. Compared to the capital city of Arcadia, this mid-sized one was positively miniscule, and their respective train stations reflected that.

The train station of Axium didn't have a roof. This meant he could see how the sun had gone almost down. It hung on the horizon, slowly creeping behind a set of mountains. Colors played across the sky like a painter had used several broad brush strokes against a canvas.

"What should we do?" Elincia asked.

Caspian thought about it, but only for a moment. *"It's too late for us to travel to Parumé. Let's rent a room for the night."*

"I guess we should, though I don't know if I can sleep right now. I feel like all we've been doing is resting."

Despite saying that, she didn't disagree with his proposal, and since their plan was set, Caspian and Elincia walked off the platform and moved into the flow of pedestrian traffic. They strode across the hard concrete floor. Dozens of bodies brushed against them, but thanks to their elf-given grace, they avoided being knocked around.

Because it was easier to speak through their bond when there was so much noise, he and Elincia kept their hands clasped, fingers laced. That said, they didn't actually need to speak through the bond to be heard. It was an excuse to hold hands, but one they readily made to themselves.

"Axium is a lot less busy than it was when I came here."

"You came here during the tournament, so that's why. This is about normal for Axium."

While Casadinia's train station was located inside of a large building, the one in Axium was outside. The numerous platforms filled with people were elevated several feet above the ground floor, and there was no roof overhead. With Caspian leading the way, the two of them walked out of the train station, passing through a set of steel gates made of intricately wrought metal.

Traffic was light in Axium—at least compared to Casadinia. Back when Elincia had arrived here, there had been hundreds—thousands, maybe even tens of thousands—of people crowding the streets, but those people had all been foreigners coming to enjoy the festival that happened before the Sorceress' Knight's Tournament. All of those people were gone. There were probably only a couple hundred people now wandering through the streets.

Caspian led the way to where they would be staying.

The Boar's Hat looked the same as it always had, a building of faded bricks, a roof that had been retiled several times, and a weathered door that needed to be replaced. The wooden stairs creaked as he and Elincia walked onto the elevated platform that led up to the entrance. Pushing the door opened, they entered the tavern.

Seeing how it was late evening, Caspian wasn't surprised to find that much of the bar was already full. Patrons were sitting at every table, in every booth, and at the bar itself. Many were laughing with the gaiety of drunkenness. Low lighting and rising smoke from large pipes and cigarettes decreased visibility. The scent of alcohol stung Caspian's nose, causing it to wrinkle.

Elincia stuck close to him as he walked up to the barkeep. He could feel several eyes trail after them as he stopped in front of the bar and placed a hand on the table. Caspian didn't know if those stares were because of him, or if it was because of Elincia, who was wearing the large cloak once again. Unlike Elincia, who walked closer as if to use him as a shield from the stares, Caspian ignored them.

"I'd like to rent out a room," Caspian said to the old man who ran the tavern. The weathered face, which reminded him of tanned leather, was the same face that he had dealt with during the tournament. The man's head was shaped kind of like a pear, and he had a large cleft in his chin.

"Didn't expect to see you here again," the barkeep grunted.

"I didn't expect to come back," Caspian replied.

"You said you wanted a room?" The old man stared at Elincia, still partially hidden behind Caspian.

"One room will be fine," Caspian said.

Another grunt. "That'll be fifty drachma."

Caspian pulled five golden coins from his pocket, dropped them on the table, and took the key that the barkeep offered him.

Drachma was the international currency used between the nations of Terraria. Made from either copper, silver, or gold, the coin's composition determined its worth. Copper coins were one drachma, silver were five, and gold was worth ten. There was also jade, which was worth one hundred drachma, but those were rare, typically only used by nobles.

"It'll be the last door on the left," the barkeep said.

Offering a brief nod to the barkeep, Caspian led Elincia up the stairs, down the hall, and to the last door on the left. The stairs creaked underneath their feet, and the hall was dimly lit. That didn't bother Caspian as he moved quickly to their room.

He entered the room, Elincia coming in behind him. Elincia's footsteps thudded along the floor as she walked further into the room while he closed the door. By the time he had turned around, she was already attempting to get out of her boots—attempting being the keyword. She was hopping around on one foot as she yanked on the boot affixed to her other.

"Let me help you out," he said to the struggling Elincia.

"Oh. Thank you."

Elincia sat down on the bed at his bidding. He knelt in front of her, grabbed her left boot, and unlaced it. As he pulled the boot off, Elincia sighed in relief and curled her toes, causing creases to appear in her knee-high socks.

Caspian did the same to her other boot.

"That feels so much better," Elincia said, stretching out her legs and wiggling her toes. They were still covered by her socks.

"Let me take these off as well," Caspian said, grabbing her left sock and slowly peeling it off. Elincia's relief was more than evident as she continued wiggling her toes around as though stretching them out. He did the same thing to her other foot, but after peeling off her sock, he didn't let go as he looked up at her. "How do you feel?"

"My feet are a little sore," she admitted, already knowing what he was really asking. "I don't like wearing boots."

Elincia almost never wore boots, preferring to either wear slippers or sandals. Elves in general did not like boots because they were too confining and didn't allow them to feel connected with nature. Even Caspian only wore them because fighting in sandals was about as smart as walking over razor blades barefoot. Sandals were too flimsy to withstand the rigors of combat and travel.

Caspian let go of her foot, stood up, and sat down on the bed. He patted his lap. "Put your feet on my lap. I'll massage them for you."

"Y-you don't have to do that," Elincia said, blushing.

"What? You're fine with me taking your boots off, but you get embarrassed by the thought of me giving you a massage?" Caspian raised an eyebrow.

A prominent pout grew on her face. "Are you teasing me?"

"Just a little," Caspian admitted.

"That's mean."

Elincia crossed her arms, pouting for a second longer before sighing. She did as he asked, scooting further up on the bed, until her back was resting against the headboard, and then lifted her legs and placed her feet on his lap.

Caspian placed his hands on her left foot and slowly applied pressure around the inner arch, feeling the knots that had come about from wearing boots. There really was a lot of tension in the muscles and tendons in her feet. Furrowing his brow in concentration, he did his best to work out those knots by rubbing them with his thumbs.

"T-that does feel really good," Elincia admitted, biting her lip in an effort not to moan. Her breathing had grown a tad heavy. Perhaps it was his imagination, but her cheeks also seemed a touch pink. He could tell she was embarrassed through their bond. However, the pleasure from his actions seemed to override her other feelings.

"The academy taught me a lot about anatomy," Caspian said as he pressed his thumbs into the middle of her foot. Elincia's small toes curled as a stifled moan escaped her lips. "While most of what we learned was which vital points we could use to kill people, we also learned how a person's body can be revitalized through the use of pressure points. The feet are particularly sensitive, and different parts of the feet correspond to different parts of the body. That's the reason foot massages have become so popular in Casadinia."

Casadinia had a number of parlors that specialize in pedicures, which came with complimentary foot massages. Many a woman gossiped about how much better they felt after going to one. Caspian had overheard those numerous conversations while wandering through the city and decided this would be a good way to help Elincia relieve the tension that came from her work.

"I-is it?" Elincia leaned her head against the headboard and closed her eyes as Caspian massaged her toes. Her toes were very small. He spread them apart to help stretch the muscles, which would release the knots and cause them to relax. Elincia bit her lip and clenched her eyes shut as her breathing turned into panting.

"It is. This is also why it's important to make sure your feet are in good condition." Caspian paused, but only because he wanted to switch topics. "Tomorrow, we'll go to the stables and rent out a carriage. Parumé is about four days hour travel on horseback, so it'll probably take us longer with a carriage. We'll have to stop at a village or two along the way there."

Caspian didn't know how many villages there were between Axium and Parumé, since there were many villages that were too small to put on a map. There was also a strong chance that one or two villages had sprang up in the time he'd been away. That said, he estimated there would be at least two or three. Parumé was located near the mountain range that separated this Axium from a wasteland.

"T-that so-sounds good."

Using the powers granted to him through their bond, Caspian chose the places on Elincia's foot that were the most sensitive. He could immediately zone in on the spots that had the greatest effect. He pushed his thumbs into those places, easing muscle tension, maximizing the pleasure... he was so caught up in helping her feel better that he didn't even realize what his actions were doing to her until it was too late.

Elincia clapped a hand over her mouth as a loud moan suddenly escaped from it. Caspian froze. It was only for a moment before he started up again by switching to her right foot. However, the longer he massaged Elincia, the more lyrical music her vocal cords produced. It was getting harder to focus as the bond sent over the overwhelming pleasure his partner was feeling, made all the worse by how Elincia's foot wiggled and squirmed within his hands.

"C-Caspian?" Elincia gasped in what sounded like an odd mixture of arousal and embarrassment. "W-what is touching my foot?"

Because his mind was clouded by Elincia's pleasure, Caspian needed a moment to respond. "Uh, my hands?"

"N-no. There… there's something else touching me."

Caspian looked down at his lap, upon which Elincia's right foot rested. Not surprisingly, her feet were tiny. It made noticing what Elincia was talking about all the easier. If he had to guess, the thing turning his pants into a tent was maybe four or five inches larger than her feet.

He stared and stared and stared, and then he looked at Elincia, who, having been staring at the exact same thing as him, peered into his eyes at the exact same time that he looked.

"Kya!"

"Ah!"

Their simultaneous screams echoed through the tavern.

***

Caspian and Elincia found themselves eating breakfast early the next morning. It wasn't much compared to what they normally ate at Sylvia's mansion, but the eggs and muffins tasted good enough. As they ate, the barkeep stared at them while cleaning a glass. Caspian ignored him. Elincia kept glancing at the man out of the corner of her eye.

"We'll rent a carriage to take us to Parumé once we finish eating." Caspian kept his eyes closed as he munched on a muffin. "It's northeast of here, so we'll leave through the north gate."

While Axium was only a mid-sized city, it was still large enough that there were four gates for people to enter and leave. This didn't include the train station, which had its own exit. The north exit was the least used, since there was nothing north of Axium save a few small villages and some farms.

"You mentioned there are other villages along the way?" Elincia said. Rumors that she was an elf hadn't spread this far yet, so she wasn't wearing a cloak to hide her face. Instead, she had Loki disguising her ears in that illusion again.

I hope the time will soon come when she doesn't need to hide her ears.

"There should be." Caspian spooned some eggs into his mouth. After swallowing, he continued. "I've checked the map in Sylvia's mansion before leaving. According to it, there are three smaller villages along the path to Parumé. Of course, those are only the villages that are large enough to be placed on the map. There might be as many as six or seven villages on the way."

"I don't know what you two are doing traveling all the way to Parumé," the barkeep said suddenly, and Caspian sighed as he realized that the man really had been listening in on their conversation. "But I wouldn't recommend going there."

"Why not?" asked Elincia.

"Rumors have been floating around all about that place," the barkeep said. He leaned forward as if to tell her a great secret. "Parumé was destroyed about twelve years ago in a bandit raid. It was supposed to be a ghost town, but someone has rebuilt it, and it's been said that several people are living there. However, there's also been a rumor that the dead were seen rising from their graves around there, too. Plus, there's been bandits operating in the forests surrounding one of the villages that you have to pass through."

This was Caspian's first-time hearing about bandits, which meant these bandits must have only made the area surrounding Parumé their base recently, or perhaps the information had been smothered by the rumor of undead wandering the villages and forests. Between these two threats, the undead were definitely larger and infinitely more frightening.

Humans feared what they could not understand. Bandits were easy to figure out. They wanted to steal your gold and valuables, so while frightening when you ran into them, they weren't terrifying to think about. Undead were different. They were not alive, so they technically should not even be able to exist, but they did, and humans knew nothing about them other than how they feasted on the flesh of the living and could only be made by necromancers and liches. They were a horrifying existence.

"We're actually here to investigate those rumors of the dead rising," Caspian informed the barkeep. "Though this is the first time I've heard about bandits roaming the area. Is there any truth to the rumors?"

The barkeep shrugged as he set a now clean glass on the table. "I don't know about the dead rising from their grave, but the bandits are real enough. Several caravans have already come under attack and have had all of the food and clothing they were carrying stolen. No one seems to have been hurt yet, which I guess is a blessing in disguise. It doesn't change the fact that lots of people have had their stuff stolen."

Just food and clothing? Not valuables? That sounded a bit weird to Caspian. Bandits often went for the valuables--money, trade goods, and sometimes even women. He'd never heard of bandits who stole just food and clothing.

"I guess we'll find out the truth when we get there." Caspian took a sip of water.

The barkeep shrugged, as if to say he'd done his part in warning them, and that anything that happened to them afterward was on their heads.

After breakfast, Caspian traveled to the stables with Elincia. It was a long walk. The train station was on the southwestern side of the city, and *The Boar's Hat* was also on that same side. The stables were on the opposite side.

Axium might not have been the size of Casadinia, or even Ashtown, but it was still large enough that walking from one side to the other would take nearly two hours.

That was fine. It gave Caspian and Elincia plenty time to think.

"What do you make of these bandits?" asked Elincia.

"I'm not sure. I mean, bandits do attack caravans, but they don't just steal the caravan's food and let the people go. Most bandits

are violent. They steal the cargo, rape the women, and usually kill everyone afterward so people don't find out about them. If that rumor is true, and there really are a group of people who are attacking caravans and letting them go, then I don't think they're bandits."

"Then what are they?"

"I don't know, and with luck, you and I won't have to find out."

It might have sounded callous, but Caspian already had a good deal of worry on his plate. Parumé, his hometown, the place where he and his mother had lived, and the village that haunted his dreams. Because his memory of his time there was so fuzzy, all he could remember was the day everyone there had been slaughtered by undead. He didn't want to worry about bandits when something like that was on his mind.

As they walked through the street, Caspian spotted a number of carriages meandering through the city. Some were basic, just a horse pulling a plane cart behind it, but a few were more intricate. One could always tell a noble's carriage from a commoner's by the ostentatiousness of their design. One of the carriages that passed them looked like a giant, white pumpkin inlaid with golden designs. Another was made from glossy wood and had purple curtains drawn tight around the windows.

MAFTs, Magically Automated Four-wheeled Transportation, were a rarity in Axium. A few wealthy nobles had them, but since Axium's primary function was to house Arcadia's Knight Academy, the city didn't have an especially booming economy.

It wasn't like Ashtown with their spirit crystal refineries, or even cities like Attore with their dozens of talented artisans. Since MAFTs were so expensive, barely anyone used them in this city. Instead, they relied on horse-drawn carriages to carry them to their destination.

The stables where one could rent a horse-drawn carriage didn't look like much, just a large, wooden stable. It seemed rickety. The wood was faded and old from being out in the sun and never having maintenance done on it. As they walked up, the scent of hay and horse manure hit their noses with its overpowering smell. Elincia wrinkled her nose.

"Not used to the smell of manure?" asked Caspian.

"N-no, I am not—are you laughing at me?"

"Sorry." Caspian chuckled. *"It's just kind of cute to see you so out of your element."*

Elincia squeaked, and Caspian decided not to tease her anymore. Tugging on her hand, he led her up to an old man with shock-white hair who was sitting on a stool in front of the stable.

"Excuse me," Caspian said. "We'd like to rent a carriage."

The old man peered at him with wizened eyes. "How long do ye plan on renting it for?"

"One month."

"That'll be five hundred drachma."

"Five hundred drachma for a single carriage is far too steep a price. One hundred drachma," Caspian countered.

"Are you trying to cheat me out of house and home? Four hundred and seventy-five drachma."

"Ha! With four hundred and seventy-five drachma, I can stay at a fine hotel for nobles. One hundred and fifty drachma."

Thus Caspian haggled with the stable master, which took a good deal of time, but even so, Caspian felt like the end result would make his stubbornness on this matter worth it. He didn't want to unnecessarily spend money if he didn't have to. Call him stingy, but there was no telling when they might need that money later on.

"Listen here, whipper snapper. I can't afford to lower my prices anymore. It's going to be three hundred and not a drachma lower."

"I'll take it."

Money exchanged hands quickly thereafter, and the old man, after counting the money in his weathered hands, pocketed the coins and blew on a whistle. A second past. Nothing happened. The old man blew on the whistle again. Another second went by. Nothing happened.

"Boy!! Don't tell me yer sleeping again! If I find that yer sleeping in the stables, so help me, I will tan yer hide until it's red!!"

"I-I wasn't sleepin', sir," a boy said as he walked out of the stables. He was a scrawny kid wearing overalls and a straw hat. His skin was tan from being out in the sun. "I swear it. I was just feeding the horses."

The old man grunted. "Tch. Like I'd believe ye. Go prepare a horse and a carriage for our customers! Have it ready quickly!"

"Y-yes, sir!" The boy saluted before running off.

"It'll take at least an hour to prepare a carriage," the old man said to them. "Come back after an hour and ye can pick it up."

"Thank you very much," Elincia said, bowing to the old man before leaving with Caspian.

"He seems like a nice man," Elincia said.

"You think so? He seemed crotchety and easily irritated to me."

"Maybe he was just grumpy about something."

"Maybe..." Caspian replied, though he didn't believe her.

Since they had about an hour to go before the carriage would be ready, Caspian took Elincia to a park with a crepe stand. It was, perhaps ironically, the same park that he had taken Elincia to after their unexpected reunion six months ago. The last time they had come there, Julius had ruined it by forcing Caspian to duel against him. It was a good thing that Julius wasn't around to ruin their time together today.

The mild weather graced Caspian with warmth as he sat down on a park bench. He offered one of the crepes to Elincia. It was filled with cream cheese, strawberries, and a host of other fruits. Caspian's, which only had strawberry and kiwi, seemed plain next to hers.

"Thank you," Elincia said seconds before biting into her crepe. She moaned in delight. "Ish sho good!"

"Remember not to talk with your mouth full," Caspian mumbled. He took a bit of his crepe. His mouth was assaulted by a burst of tantalizing flavors. These crepes really were delicious. He could see why Elincia went crazy over them.

After eating his crepe, Caspian glanced at the park. Numerous familiar trees sat upon the grass. Children ran through those trees, which currently did not have their leaves due to the season. Even so, the mild weather of Arcadia pervaded Axium just as it did in

Casadinia.

Elincia touched his hand. *"Are you remembering what happened here?"*

"They never did find Julius." Caspian looked up at the sky. *"I wonder what happened to him."*

"Worried?"

Caspian shook his head. *"Just curious. Julius isn't the kind of person I would worry over, even if he really was in danger."*

"I guess not."

Caspian could tell through their bond that Elincia wasn't quite pleased with his answer, but it was the only one he could give. Julius had been a thorn in his side. The man had used every opportunity he could to humiliate him. He would not cry over that man even if he discovered that Julius had been killed.

"Are you ready? They should be about finished preparing our carriage," Caspian said.

"Yes." Elincia finished off her crepe. *"I'm all done."*

The two of them left the park and traveled back to the staples. Caspian was correct. The carriage was indeed ready and waiting for them upon their return, though it wasn't quite what Caspian had expected when he had first bartered for it. Smaller than most of the carriages he had seen, this one consisted of a flatbed in the back and a small bench up front. It seemed sturdy enough, and the wheels didn't look like they would roll off the moment they started moving, but he had expected something more.

"This is one of the better carriages we have," the old man said, his weathered jowls flapping. "Remember, if ye break this carriage, yer going to be buying it."

"We understand," Caspian said.

"Thank you for letting us rent it from you." Elincia bowed to the old man in gratitude.

"Heheh." The old man seemed a bit tickled that Elincia would show such kindness. "Ye've got a fine girl here. Make sure ye take care of her."

"I will," Caspian said as Elincia blushed a pretty shade of red.

Caspian put their luggage into the flatbed, climbed onto the bench up front and, sitting down, he turned and held out a hand for Elincia. After pulling her up, he took the reins.

This carriage was only being drawn by one horse, but considering he had only paid three hundred drachma, he guessed it couldn't be helped.

"Ready?" he asked Elincia.

She nodded. "Yes!"

With a whip of the reigns, Caspian got the cart moving. The horse neighed as it pulled them onto the paved road.

Despite there not being many MAFTs, there was still a good deal of traffic from other horse-drawn carriages. Since he wasn't experienced with driving a carriage, Caspian acted more cautiously than he usually did.

They passed by numerous houses, shops, taverns, and other buildings. In the distance, Caspian could glimpse the colosseum where the tournament had taken place six months ago. It looked like they had rebuilt it. He'd heard a rumor that Sylvia had called together a group of sorceresses who specialized in the summoning of earth spirits to do this.

Several arches marked the northern gate. Each archway was held up by a pair of large columns. When they reached the front, Caspian stopped the carriage. There was a Peacekeeper outpost sitting to his left. They needed to clear this checkpoint before they would be allowed to leave.

"State your name and business," a bored-looking young man said with a yawn. He was a big man with a square jaw and no eyebrows on his thick brow-ridges. Caspian thought he looked familiar, but it was hard to tell.

"I am Caspian, and this is Elincia," he said. "We're leaving for Parumé to investigate something on behalf of the Sorceress Council."

"Caspian?!" the young man squawked. "Woah! It really is you! It's been a long time, hasn't it? I haven't seen you since the tournament."

Caspian frowned. "Do I know you?"

Perhaps having not expected such a response, though Caspian couldn't imagine why anyone would have expected anything else, the young man tripped and face planted onto the ground. He clambered back to his feet, holding his bloody nose. While he seemed exasperated, he also looked resigned.

"I guess it's not surprising you don't remember me," he mumbled. "My name is Chronux. I was one of Julius' friends back at the academy."

"Oh! Now I remember you!"

Looking at him more closely now, Caspian could see why he looked so familiar. Chronux was a giant man, perhaps not as large as Julius had been with his bulging muscles, but certainly bigger than most people. Even though he and Elincia were sitting on an elevated carriage, Chronux was so tall they were still at eye level with him.

"Even after becoming a sorceress's knight, you haven't changed," Chronux said with a resigned grumble.

Caspian's answer was a shrug. "I'm not sure why you would expect me to change. Anyway, are we allowed to go now?"

"You're free to leave." Chronux waved his hand. "Just let me give you this chance to warn you to be careful. There have been numerous bandit sightings up north. Also, if you're going to Parumé, then you should be prepared. While no one really knows what exactly is happening there, the rumor is that undead are infesting the land."

"I know," Caspian said. "That's what we're here to investigate."

Cracking the reigns again, Caspian directed their carriage through the gate. There was nothing but open plain after that.

Ruudon was a rural province. Farmlands, grassy fields, and the occasional forest were what made up a majority of the landscape. At that moment, Caspian and Elincia were passing mostly farmlands. There was a meandering river that ran through Axium, and so several farms had been built along the river's edge. They used irrigation canals to help the wheat fields and other vegetable gardens grow.

"You know, I never got to see much of the Ruudon Province when I came here for the tournament," Elincia said, turning her head left and right to observe their surroundings. Her eyes were sparkling.

If her ears hadn't been hidden by Loki's illusion, he was sure they'd have been wiggling as well.

"You never did leave Axium during that time," Caspian agreed. "Still, you should have been able to see at least glimpses during the train ride."

"I was too excited by the prospect seeing you to notice the scenery when I first arrived in Axium," Elincia admitted, the mildest of blushes gracing her cheeks.

Caspian smiled. He didn't say anything, but he would admit that her words made him feel, well, special. That he could make her so excited that she didn't even notice the scenery, which he knew she would have normally been curious about, pleased him.

Meters to their left, the gently flowing river shone like a brilliant blue diamond in the sunlight. It would be awhile before they reached their first destination. He figured they had best enjoy this peace and scenery while they could.

After all, there was no telling what awaited them when they finally reached Parumé.

Chapter 3

According to the map that Caspian had, the first village on their way to Parumé was an even smaller village known as Exiguus. Caspian didn't know anything about the village—it hadn't existed when he was living in this area—but the map said that to get there, they needed to travel through a small forest, which was exactly what he and Elincia were doing right then.

The forest that he drove the carriage through didn't have a name. If it did, then he didn't know it. All he knew was the sparse sprinkling of light that rained upon them through the canopy caused leaf-shaped patterns of light to dance along the forest floor. Noises from animals echoed in the distance, beyond his line of sight; toads croaked, crickets chirped, owls hooted, and other sounds that he couldn't place melded together to create a natural music.

Accompanying the music as he followed the small dirt road through the forest was Elincia's breathing. The soft inhale and exhale of her breath sang in his ear, a beautiful melody that let him know she was at peace.

His sorceress, best friend, and the most important person in his life all in one had fallen asleep some time ago. She was leaning against him, wrapped in her cloak, her head on his shoulder. Although he couldn't see anything underneath the cloak, he could feel her thighs touching his through the fabric. Thanks to their physical contact, he could also feel her through their bond.

Elincia was dreaming. About him. About them. He could see in her mind the things she wanted them to do, to experience.

Some of these things were not appropriate for children.

He stared at the hands that were cutting up several vegetables and putting them into a pot of boiling stew. They were delicate hands. The long fingers carried a femininity that he knew he did not possess. A hum escaped from parted lips, soft and beautiful, a lilting melody that soothed all who heard it—including him.

This is… Elincia's dream?

It was obvious, really. These hands were not his. Having spent many hours watching her, admiring her, he knew that these hands belonged to Elincia.

I must be experiencing this dream through Elincia's eyes.

As the hands that were not his continued preparing a meal inside of what he could only guess was a kitchen, the clicking of an opening door echoed to his—Elincia's—ears. The cutting stopped, a lid was placed over the boiling pot, and his vision bounced as hurried footsteps sounded out in his ears. He—or rather, Elincia— rushed through a door and down a hallway. She stopped in front of a door.

Someone was standing there.

If he could have, Caspian would have blinked when he found himself staring at himself. This Caspian looked exactly like him, right down to the very last detail. The difference was that he didn't have his sword, and he wasn't wearing the clothing that he had gotten from Cassidy back when he was acting as Erica's temporary knight. Instead, he was wearing a pair of sturdy black pants, a white collared shirt, a red vest, and sandals. There was a bandolier slung around his shoulder, a quiver full of arrows attached to it.

"Caspian..." Even though he knew, logically, that it was Elincia's lips moving and not his, it still felt weird to hear her voice coming from what felt like his mouth. "How was your hunt?"

The Caspian in front of the door grinned. "It went well. I caught several deer and even a few rabbits. I've already prepared them and put them in the cooler. They'll be good to have during the winter season."

The Caspian that was him but not him—Dream Caspian—took off his sandals. That was another thing that let him know this wasn't him. He didn't wear sandals since they weren't good for combat. As Dream Caspian did that, the real Caspian felt a smile tug at Elincia's lips.

"I'm so glad to hear that! Oh, dinner will be ready in just a bit."

Dream Caspian nodded and, stepping up to her, he peered down at Elincia's much smaller body with a mysterious gleam in his eyes. "Sounds good. How's Elaine doing? Is she out playing with her friends still?"

Scintillating golden hair swayed in front of his face as Elincia shook her head. "She came home a little while ago. Right now she's sleeping in her room."

"Then that means no one is around to interrupt us."

The words had scarcely left Dream Caspian's mouth when he moved, pinning Elincia to the wall with his more masculine body. One of his hands rested against her waist. The other was against the wall. Meanwhile, Dream Caspian had claimed Elincia's lips in a heated kiss.

Caspian didn't know how he felt about kissing himself, even though he knew that he was seeing Elincia's dreams from her perspective and not actually kissing himself. Even so, it was still creepy. It became especially bad when Dream Caspian's tongue penetrated Elincia's mouth. It became even worse when a low, arousing moan erupted from Elincia and a gentle, simmering heat pooled in her loins.

"Oh!"

Elincia gasped when Dream Caspian removed his mouth from hers to attack her neck. He trailed kisses along her skin, nibbled on her collarbone, then went back up and tenderly took her ears between his teeth. The moaning grew louder as Caspian grew more embarrassed.

It was weird to feel Elincia's arousal. There was a heat inside of her that he could feel as though it was his own. What's more, the panties that Elincia was wearing were growing damp. Caspian didn't think anyone would blame him for being disturbed by all this.

"Ca-Caspian, we can't do this right now!" Elincia said, though the real Caspian, who currently had a backseat to everything she was thinking and feeling, knew that she had no real desire to stop. Not only were her protests half-hearted, but she had grabbed Dream Caspian's rear end. Caspian could actually feel Dream Caspian's butt as though Elincia's fingers were his own.

Hmm… does my ass really feel this hard?

"It'll be fine," Dream Caspian said as one of his hands slid underneath her dress and cupped her breast.

Caspian felt a jolt, both pleasant and loathsome, travel down his spine. Even if this was a dream, he didn't like this other Caspian touching Elincia. It was a very odd feeling to feel jealous of himself.

"B-but dinner…"

"Can wait. Right now, the only thing I want is you."

That seemed to be the limit of Elincia's resistance because in the next moment, she was kissing Dream Caspian with just as much vigor as he was kissing her. Elincia's hands ran through his hair. She nibbled on his lower lip. One of her legs had come up and hooked around Caspian's, sliding up and down as though trying to rub off his pants.

The pants came off seconds later. Clothes were sent flying through the air, and Caspian could only watch with a growing sense of horror as Elincia's dream turned into an erotic nightmare.

Back in the real world, Caspian could only switch to a one-handed hold on the reins and use his now free hand to pinch the bridge of his nose. He was so embarrassed by Elincia's dream that he felt like there was enough blood rushing to his face that it might come out of his nose. No doubt his cheeks were red enough to be mistaken for a forest fire.

Despite how he felt like someone had slammed a bludgeoning into his head, Elincia's dream made him think. Was this what she wanted from him? It seemed like her dreams were a byproduct of her desire to further their relationship. That was what Caspian was assuming, at any rate.

Maybe it would be a good idea to be a bit more aggressive. It seems like Ele wants me to take a more active role in becoming physically intimate with her.

That was going to be tough. Caspian wanted that intimacy, but neither he nor Elincia had any experience with romance outside of each other. What's more, he'd spent the last several years at an all-boys academy. It had been a total sausage fest. Could he really pull off that kind of suave act that he had seen in her dream? He didn't know. He didn't think he could.

Caspian glanced at the trees that his horse-drawn carriage was slowly moving past. It had gotten pretty quiet for some reason. He could no longer hear any noise from the animals, almost as if they had all gone silent at the same. A strange tension hung in the air that hadn't been there before. It was almost like—

—The air whistled.

Reacting with reflexes honed by experience, Caspian reached out and grabbed the arrow before it could pierce Elincia's shoulder. It was an unusual arrow. Unlike most, this one didn't have a sharp point but a rounded one. The composition was also strange. It wasn't even made of metal.

Is this wood?

"Ele! Wake up!"

Maybe she had heard the sharpness in his voice, or perhaps the way his heart skyrocketed had alerted her to the danger, but Elincia snapped awake near instantly.

"Caspian! What's going on?"

"We're under attack! Get ready to summon a spirit!"

Several more arrows came out from within the trees. Caspian had no choice but to let go of the reigns. He cursed as the horse neighed loudly and bolted, but he couldn't do anything about that. Leaping to his feet, he unsheathed his sword and swatted each and every arrow out of the air with pinpoint precision. No clang of metal echoed as he cut the arrows down. These wooden arrows with their rounded arrowheads wouldn't even be able to kill them, but they would sting.

"Jörð! Please protect us!"

The earth shook, a loud rumbling filled Caspian's ears, and then, like daemons rising from the muck, large stone creatures climbed out of the earth—or so it seemed. It would have been more accurate to say they were beings made from the earth. All of the ground moved toward them, gathering to create them, forming a crater around where they stood. The earth, grass and dirt and rocks, coagulated together, grew bigger, and took on several shapes.

Golems. Massive creatures made of earth. Caspian had only seen them once before, during the time when he had been acting as Erica's temporary knight what felt like a lifetime ago. Saying that, it would have been wrong to compare those golems to these. Those were small. These towered far over his and Elincia's heads. He judged them to be at least two meters tall. There were four in total.

As one, the golems stamped their feet onto the ground, which caused the earth to shake again. The ground split apart. Trees broke underneath the assault as the very earth they sat upon was upheaved. Strangely enough, despite the destruction happening all around them, Caspian and Elincia were perfectly safe.

"Did that get them?" Elincia wondered.

Her question was answered when several arrows flew from within the underbrush. Caspian stood defensively in front of Elincia, prepared to protect her. She wasn't the target. The arrows struck the golem on their left, and then exploded with the brilliance of three suns.

If golems could roar, Caspian was sure this one would have done just that. Massive chunks of earth flew everywhere as the golem was struck in the face, chest, and left leg. The creation's head blew off. Its chest exploded like it had been struck with a cannonball. Being the weakest part of its body, the golem's leg disappeared entirely, and since it no longer had two legs, it crashed to the ground.

More arrows slammed into the other three golems. Elincia screamed, but Caspian grabbed her arm and pulled her off the carriage.

"Command the golems to shake the earth," he instructed.

"Please make these golems cause an earthquake, Jörð!"

Only two golems were left, but they still followed her orders to the letter. They stamped on the ground. The entire world shook, fissures spread from where their feet had struck the ground, and even more trees were felled as the earth became reshaped.

Caspian didn't wait around to see what would happen next. He pulled Elincia behind him, using the confusion caused by the golems to hopefully escape. It meant abandoning the carriage, which sucked, but that couldn't be helped. He would pay the old man for the carriage when they arrived back at Axium.

More explosions shook the air behind them, causing heat to wash over their backs and buffet their hair. The golems wouldn't last much longer.

"How is your mana?" Caspian asked.

"F-fine," Elincia breathed. "Those golems don't cost much, and I'm not using Loki to hide my ears, so I have plenty of magic left over."

Loki's illusion was a constant drain on her mana reserves. Without that illusion, she had nearly four times more mana available to her.

"Good. We might need it."

"What?"

Caspian pushed Elincia to the ground when several arrows shot out from within the trees, aimed at their heads. Spinning around a full

360 degrees, he called out, "Halkaista!" which created a strong cutting blade that sliced through even air. The arrows didn't stand a chance. They were destroyed instantly.

"Now, Ele!"

Still on the ground, Elincia seemed able to determine what he wanted. She pressed her palms against the hard surface and shouted, "Jörð! Please come here and help us!"

Nearly a dozen more arrows rained down on them, but each one was blocked, not by Caspian, but by her.

She appeared from within the earth, a woman with skin several shades darker than most Arcadians. It was a dark brown that almost bordered on black. Midnight hair drifted on a breeze. She wasn't wearing any clothing, which meant her body, which seemed to have been designed to embody perfection, was displayed for all to see. Her large breasts were round and firm, her stomach was flat and toned, and her hips were likewise wide and seemed perfect for childbearing. Dark brown eyes surveyed the area, calm, collected, almost heedless of the fact that Caspian was getting an eye full.

An arrow with a bomb attached to it shot at her head. A wall of earth rose up before it could strike. It exploded against the wall but was unable to break through. Jörð then stretched out a hand, long fingers almost lovingly touching the wall.

Caspian nearly tripped when the wall suddenly turned into a massive fist that shot forward like a bullet fired from a musket. It slammed through the underbrush. A scream of pain was heard seconds later, followed by a messy crunching sound like someone's bones were being shattered.

That seemed to be a signal of some kind. Five people leapt out from the underbrush and charged at them. Perhaps they had realized that they couldn't win like this, hiding within the foliage and attacking from a distance. Then again, charging in when they were up against a spirit was even dumber than hanging back.

Jörð tapped her foot on the ground, and suddenly, five earthen pillars grew from the surrounding forest floor at speeds quicker than Caspian imagined possible. They were all aimed at one of the people charging at them. Most of them were dodged, their attackers swerving around it, but one of them couldn't move out of the way and got plowed in the face. That person was sent flying.

In order to feel less useless, Caspian launched himself into the fray. His first enemy blocked his swing with a dagger that he held in a reverse grip. Already experienced with dagger users, Caspian didn't bother locking blades.

He retracted his sword, kicked out their shin, and then punted them in the head after they had been knocked off balance. The dagger wielder's head snapped back with an almost audible *cracking* sound. He dropped like a sack of bricks.

Standing on Elincia's opposite side, protecting her from attacks, Jörð continued manipulating the earth. Her movements were almost like a dance. Her arms moved and the earth rose. She touched a foot upon the ground and the ground came alive. Not only did the walls she raised protect her, but they also protected Elincia from potential bowmen.

Caspian was forced to take his eyes off Jörð. Another person attacked him. Like the others, this person was covered from head to toe in a black cloak. They had no hood, but the bandages they wore wrapped around their head like a mummy and kept him from seeing their face. Only a few strands of grayish blond hair stuck out. Clasped firmly in their hand was a rusted broadsword.

Backpedaling, Caspian avoided the first swing, and then he moved in and raised his blade to block the second. *Clang!* Like the clashing of thunder in the distance, their swords rang out as they met, but Caspian had no intention of letting this become a stalemate. He took another step forward, causing his opponent stumble backward. Sadly, Caspian couldn't take advantage of this. His foe caught himself and leapt backwards, out of his range.

Caspian didn't attack. These people were probably the bandits that had been spoken of back in Axium, but they didn't attack like bandits. They were being too merciful. A real bandit would have gone in for the kill from the moment this battle started. They also would have been exuding a lot more bloodlust.

"Who are you?" Caspian demanded. "Why did you attack us?"

"You're going to regret coming here. Mark my words," the person said, their voice higher pitched than he had expected. His opponent sounded like a woman.

He wasn't given much time to think about this further, for a second later, the woman whistled.

It seemed like that was a signal of some kind. All of the people who had been fighting leapt to their feet and disappeared into the trees. Caspian, in desperation, tossed his dagger at the woman, but she moved backwards into the foliage, her figure fading like a ghost. His blade went right through her as though she didn't exist, continuing on and impaling a tree several meters away.

"Damn, it looks like they got away," he muttered. He was upset, but he also knew there wasn't much he could do. Unlike a pureblood elf, he could not commune with nature to follow them.

Turning around, Caspian found Elincia kneeling on the ground, sweat covering her body and her breathing heavy. He rushed over to her side and knelt next to her.

"Ele, are you okay?" he asked as he placed a hand on her back.

"Y-yes," Elincia muttered. "I'm just not used to summoning Jörð."

Jörð was a spirit of the earth, much like Gaia, and like the Grecian spirit, Jörð was often considered the personification of Terraria. It was she who controlled all-natural aspects of the world. Her powers were such that many considered her to be on par with Gaia.

"She is a powerful spirit." Caspian stood up and held out his hand. "Summoning her must take a lot more mana than most spirits —not that I can't see why you summoned her."

"I figured she would be able to protect us the best, since we're in a forest." Elincia grabbed his hand and allowed him to pull her up. "I just didn't realize that summoning her here would exhaust me like this."

"Can you walk?"

Elincia shook her head. "My legs aren't moving. I think I might have pulled something while we were running."

"Then I guess there's nothing to it." Caspian hooked one of his arms under Elincia's legs as the other went around her shoulder. The blonde elf squawked as he lifted her into a bridal carry.

"C-Caspian!"

"Since you're too tired to walk, I'm going to carry you the rest of the way," he said. "You don't have a problem with that, right?"

"Um… no." Elincia squirmed in his grip as her arms went around his neck. "This… is actually kinda… nice."

"Good to know. Maybe I'll carry you like a princess more often."

"Caspian!"

Despite the situation, Caspian laughed as he restarted their journey to the next town.

***

They did not make it to the next town before nightfall. Not only was Elincia too exhausted to walk on her own, but Caspian became more tired the longer he carried her through the forest. To make matters worse, it had gotten dark outside. While this rarely deterred an elf because they had incredible vision even at night, Caspian didn't know what kind of monsters might be lurking within this darkness.

We don't have our luggage anymore, Elincia has used too much mana, and there's no telling when those people who ambushed us might come back. As these thoughts occurred to him, a small grimace came unbidden to his face. *This is a pleasant situation.*

"I'm sorry," Elincia's voice reached him through the bond.

He looked down. Elincia was still in his arms, being carried like a newlywed woman or a recently awakened princess from a fairy tale. Her head was resting against his shoulder. Her arms were wrapped around his neck. Caspian could barely contain his shudder as her hot breath hit his skin through the fabric of his shirt.

Her leg had become slightly swollen, showing that she had indeed strained her muscle, but she could heal it once her depleted mana reserves were restored.

"Don't apologize for something that isn't your fault."

"But—"

"What happened isn't your fault. This was just one of those things that's beyond our ability to control. We had no way of knowing that the bandits would attack us, and even though we took some precautions, it's not like we could have done anything against a larger force that knows the terrain better than we do. It'll be alright. We'll figure something out."

Elincia was silent for a moment. Then…

"Thank you."

Caspian smiled but didn't speak as he observed their surroundings, searching for a place where they could sleep. He had traveled off the road. Trees crowded around them, but his natural elven grace allowed him to move between them with relative ease, hopping over roots, avoiding vines and branches. Even if it was dark, and the trees and foliage were so thick he could only see several meters in any direction, his eyesight was enough that he could pick out greater details than the average human.

Unfortunately, as much as Caspian searched, there was nowhere for them to sleep. This place had nothing, no caves, no hollowed-out trees, not even a glade that they could sit in. It was just a forest.

"Sorry, Ele. It looks like we're going to have to spend the night right here."

"I don't mind... as long as I'm with you, I can deal with anything."

"That's kind of you to say, but I wish you didn't have to deal with something like this."

Caspian set Elincia down against a tree. Her ankle had become large and red by this point. It was more than a simple sprain. He was surprised she was taking it so well, since Elincia was not as inured to pain as he was. If they still had their luggage, he could have treated the injury with the medical kit he'd brought along, but…

He sat down under the same tree. With their backs pressed against the trunk, the smooth wood sending cool chills down his spine, Caspian had a free moment to feel a sense of self-loathing. His handling of this situation had been terrible. He should have done more, should have been more prepared.

Had D'artagnan been in this position, there was no doubt in his mind that Sylvia's knight would've done a far better job than Caspian. He wouldn't have lost their horse. He wouldn't have been forced to abandon their luggage. D'artagnan would have—

"Please stop that." A voice entered his mind. *"Stop degrading yourself. None of what you said just now is true."*

"But it is. If D'artagnan was here, he—"

"I doubt he would've fared any better."

"Do you... really think so?"

"I do." Elincia shifted her body until she was leaning on him. She hugged his arm and snuggled into his side. She must have really been exhausted, otherwise there's no way she would've done this without becoming embarrassed. *"You have a bad habit of putting others on a pedestal and undermining your own strength."*

Caspian didn't think that was the case. He was just being realistic. Even now, he could still remember how powerful D'artagnan and the other knights had been at the tournament. D'artagnan had fought against the giant form of Gaia without aid. He had fought and stood his ground, not conceding an inch until Sylvia had been ready to deliver the finishing blow. His performance had astounded Caspian, and it made him realize how far he still had to go before he could reach that height, the pinnacle of knightly strength.

"That may be so but fighting against a creature of that size is different from fighting against a bunch of individuals. I doubt he could have done that well against multiple opponents." Once more, Elincia determined what he was thinking through their bond and cut his thoughts down.

A thankful smile made Caspian's lips twitch of their own accord. *"There's no winning with you, is there?"*

"Not in matters like this. I won't let you degrade yourself. You are my knight and someone I've admired since we were young. If you believe that you're worthless, then what does that say about me, the

one who believes you're irreplaceable and precious? You are not worthless. You never will be."

Her words were like a panacea for his heart, a healing balm that did more to sooth his troubled thoughts than any elixir ever could.

He didn't know why he was so under confident these days. Back at the academy, he had always put up a strong front, never backing down when people tried to push him around, never putting up with other people's crap. He had even picked fights with teachers when they tried to disgrace and humiliate him in front of the class. Despite dealing with bullying from teachers, students, and faculty alike, Caspian had clawed his way up to the top and been ranked as the second strongest swordsman in school. He should have been proud in his abilities.

But he wasn't.

Watching people like D'artagnan day in and day out, seeing how strong the other knights were, it made him feel inadequate. Even though he pushed himself to be better every day, it sometimes felt like he would never amount to anything. However...

Elincia believes in me...

She didn't let him get away with saying bad things about himself. Whenever he had something self-deprecating to say, she would say something uplifting, encouraging. It made him want to change.

He wanted to become a better person, a more confident person. Caspian didn't want to be the man who hid behind a facade of fake confidence like he had in the past, like his academy days. He wanted to become someone who could proudly stand beside Elincia.

I need to gain real confidence, the kind that comes from experience instead of the fake bravado I had when I was a student.

He glanced down. Elincia had fallen asleep. Her eyes were closed, long blond lashes making her attractive face all the more alluring. The gentle breathing released from her parted mouth and the warmth of her body against his lulled him into a sense of sleepiness. Caspian could do nothing to fight against his exhaustion, which hit him like a train.

Sighing, he closed his hands, his body relaxing as he gave into Elincia's warmth. Time stood still… for a time.

It felt like Caspian had barely fallen asleep before he was forced awake again. As a light sleeper, even the softest of noises could wake him up. What had woken him up this time was a noise that he recognized, perhaps instinctively, as dangerous. *Crunch-snap!* It was the sound of someone crunching twigs and branches beneath them as they walked, and it was getting closer.

Caspian kept his eyes closed, forced his breathing to remain calm, and listened. *Crunch-snap!* The sound was coming from his left and slightly in front of him. *Crunch-snap! Snap snap!* It was coming closer. Slow and ponderous steps, as if the person was stumbling toward him in a drunken stupor.

What should I do? Is this person an enemy? Could it be someone from that group who attacked us the previous day? No. If it was, I'm sure they would have attacked from a distance. Their ambush had been well planned. They wouldn't attack like this. That means it's someone else, but who?

Cracking his eyes open just a bit, Caspian glanced in the direction that the noise was coming from. *Crunch crunch snap!* Bare feet hit the ground with a cumbersome density that seemed unnatural. It was like the person had lost all feelings in their feet. What's more, the feet that suddenly appeared in his vision were rotting and decrepit, like the feet of a corpse that had been dug up from a grave.

It couldn't be…

Caspian glanced further up. Decaying legs were covered in tattered jeans, sun spotted skin that had more in common with overripe fruit than flesh. He looked up further. Just like the legs, the skin of their torso was exposed because of the numerous holes in the shirt, which barely clung to the body, hanging on precariously by a few threads. Dead, rotting flesh revealed itself beneath the clothing. There were several places where the skin had been peeled off to reveal the muscles underneath, but even those were yellow and rotting.

Then Caspian finally looked at the person's face. White eyes that had no pupil. A slack jawed mouth with the kind of deformity that let him know it was broken. Peeling skin. Sagging flesh. This wasn't a person.

It was an undead.

Realizing the kind of danger he and Elincia were in, Caspian sent a shout through their bond.

"Wake up, Ele! We're under attack!"

Elincia woke up with a startled jerk. He slipped from her grasp after that, standing up, grabbing his sword, unsheathing it, and attacking in one smooth motion.

Undead were not intelligent creatures, nor were they fast or strong. As nothing more than a reanimated corpse, they could only obey simple commands, so doing something as complex as dodging was impossible for them. That was why Caspian's sword sheared through its neck with such ease. As the head rolled to the ground and the body followed, Elincia stood to her feet blinking several times as she stared at the creature now lying headless at Caspian's feet.

"That… Caspian, did you—"

"I didn't kill anyone," Caspian said. "That thing was an undead."

Elincia sucked in a breath. "Then that means…"

"Right." Caspian nodded. "The necromancer must be nearby. How much mana do you have?"

Hesitating before she answered, Caspian got the sense that she was checking her reserves to see how much power she had left. "I'm not at full power, but I should be fine so long as I don't do a full summoning."

Elincia's power was completely different from a normal sorceress. Instead of chanting an Aria and allowing a spirit to inhabit her body, she called spirits from their celestial plane of existence to this world. Doing so had its benefits, but it also had many downsides.

When a spirit was summoned to this world, they could use their full power, but it came at the cost of the summoner's mana. Each spell a spirit used drained the summoner, and since spirits required a lot of mana to use spells, Elincia's mana would be drained quickly.

And, of course, there was also the fact that just keeping a spirit on this plane constantly drained one's mana.

In short, if Elincia wasn't careful, she could exhaust her reserves before she knew it.

Caspian nodded. "Stick behind me. Keep your eyes peeled. If you see anyone, tell me their location. With luck, you won't have to use do any summoning."

"Right." Elincia bent down and touched her swollen leg with a hand. "Eir, please heal this."

A soft glow enveloped her leg. The swelling and redness disappeared. Elincia stood back up.

"Let's go," Caspian said.

They moved slowly through the forest, keeping their eyes open and their ears peeled. Caspian put all of his concentration into his senses. He could feel Elincia behind him, hear her frightened footsteps and her shaky breathing. The forest was quiet. None of the nocturnal animals that should have been awake and making noise were around. It was a sign that they were not alone.

Crunch! Snap!

A twig snapped on their left. Caspian spun around just as an undead emerged from between the trees. He reacted quickly, closing the distance between them in a mere instant, his sword swinging.

There was a moment of resistance. Then, as if he was cutting through a fruit, his blade sliced through the flesh of the undead's neck. Its head rolled off of its body. It hit the ground and tumbled away, and then the body fell, collapsing on the ground.

"Caspian! On your right!"

The shout made Caspian spin once more, and he quickly looked in the direction Elincia indicated. Another undead had appeared. This one was dealt with in the same manner as the first.

Undead were essentially humans that had been reanimated. Their brains were activated using a sort of parasitic magic that allowed the caster to control the body like it was a marionette. Since all of the undead's movements were still controlled through the brain, the best method to exterminate them was to cut off the head.

"Let's run for it," Caspian said. Elincia nodded.

With no way of knowing how many undead there were or the location of the necromancer responsible, they were left with few options. In fact, they really only had one option if they wanted to get out of this alive. Get out of the forest and find shelter where the undead couldn't reach them.

Their footsteps were ominous in how loud they were as he and Elincia crushed twigs and rustled leaves underfoot. The sound pounded in Caspian's ears. Accompanying their flight was their heavy breathing. Even Caspian, who wasn't exactly tired, could feel his own breath coming out in ragged gasps.

Adrenaline raced through Caspian as they ran. Behind him, Elincia nearly stumbled, but he grabbed her hand and kept her from falling. They couldn't afford to slow down. Not now.

Several undead appeared before them. They came out from behind trees, appeared from within thick bushes, and stumbled toward them like puppets being pulled along by threads.

Caspian cut them down. Like wheat before the scythe, he sliced through them all, his sword singing a song of constant death. Yet no matter how many he killed, there were always more coming out. It was like they were an endless horde.

"On our left!"

Caspian turned and cut down an undead that had been sneaking up on their left. Its head left its body. It fell to the ground. They kept running.

"The right now!"

Caspian spun. His blade flashed. Another undead became headless.

What's going on here?! He screamed at himself. *They're showing up way too quickly! It's almost like they're converging on us, but that shouldn't be possible!*

Undead were not intelligent enough to use tactics; they were mindless creatures that ran on little more than instinct. Yet he and Elincia were clearly being surrounded. Undead showed up in all directions. Left. Right. Behind. In front. Their numbers increased with every passing second like they were converging on their location. If this kept up, they would become so overrun that not even summoning a spirit would save them.

As if someone had heard their plight, an arrow shot out from the darkness and pierced the skull of an undead that tried to attack Elincia from behind. It fell to the ground with a boneless thud. Caspian looked at where the arrow had come from.

There was someone standing there.

"Hurry up, you idiots! Run!" the familiar cloaked figure shouted at them. It was one of the people who'd attacked them earlier in the day. Judging from the pitch and timber of their voice, this person was a woman.

Caspian didn't know why the person who had attacked them was now helping them, but he didn't care, not right then. If this was a trap, he would gladly walk into it. Their priority in that moment was getting away from the endless horde of undead.

"Ele, do you have enough mana to build a wall?"

"Um, yes! I should."

"Then do. Build a wall behind us."

"Right! Jörð!"

Summoned by her words, a massive chunk of earth suddenly jutted from the ground. Trees were upheaved, the gravel shifted, everything made way for the giant wall that now stood between them and numerous undead. This didn't solve all of their problems. There were still undead coming from their left and right, but with one less side to worry about, Caspian easily took care of the ones that came at them.

"Hurry up!" the cloaked person shouted again.

Caspian and Elincia rushed past the cloaked figure, and Caspian belatedly realized that this person wasn't alone. There were several other people with her. He hadn't noticed them at first because he'd been so focused on the woman. While she was weaponless, the others were wielding bows with flames on the tips.

"Fire!" the woman shouted after he and Elincia had rushed past her.

Several dozen arrows shot into the darkness. Not all of them hit their targets, but even when they didn't, something still caught fire. The undead who were shot lit up as the oils and fats in their decomposed bodies combusted.

This didn't stop them at first. Undead did not have active pain receptors. Even so, as their internal organs, including their brains, were consumed by the flames, the undead slowly fell to the ground and stayed there.

"Come on, everyone!" the woman shouted again. "We're retreating—that includes you two! Move it!"

Elincia's grip on his hand tightened. *"Caspian?"*

"There's no choice. Let's follow them for now."

As he and Elincia followed the woman who was giving orders, Caspian noticed that all of the cloaked figures were surrounding them. His nerves shot up. His spine tingled. The desire to feel his fingers wrap around the hilt of his blade was strong, but he resisted. Nothing good would come from making any confrontational moves right now.

They moved in silence. A heaviness filled the air, tense and thick, like smoke clogging the inside of a burning building. Caspian and Elincia didn't speak, but only on the outside.

"We're surrounded. No doubt they did this on purpose. If we make a run, they'll probably shoot us."

"What should we do?"

"There's not much we can do. I doubt they'll kill us, though. Those arrows they had used on us had a rounded tip and were made of wood instead of steel. Vastly different from what they used on these undead. They're clearly not out to kill anyone."

Caspian was surprised when, after several minutes of walking, he realized that they weren't being attacked by undead. He soon found out why when he looked at the forest floor. A cornucopia of corpses lay sprawled along the ground.

There wasn't much blood, but undead didn't have blood flowing through them, so it made sense. Even so, the rancid stench wafting from their decaying bodies was enough to make him cringe.

"There are so many of them," Elincia's voice through their bond was a mere whisper.

"It looks like an entire village's worth of people," Caspian agreed.

Did this mean that Exiguus had also been attacked by the necromancer? And what about these people? Who were they? Caspian had so many questions. Half of the reason he was even willing to follow these people, outside of the fact that they were surrounded, was because he was hoping to get some answers.

Eventually coming upon an area that was thick with trees and vines, Caspian and Elincia were forced to close ranks with the others. Brambles smacked into his face. Branches scraped his cheeks. He almost choked on a vine that nearly became wrapped around his throat. However, eventually, after following the leader of these people, they came upon a small clearing in which a tiny house sat.

To call it a house might have been overstating things. It was so small that Caspian could barely imagine more than ten people being able to fit inside at any given time. Wooden beams were stuck together with nails. The different sizes of each beam made the whole thing appear as though it had been cobbled together from spare parts.

"Come on, you two." The leader gestured for them. "You're coming inside. We need to talk. Alone."

Several of the cloaked figures started. One of them even took a step forward and said, "but Momma, surely you don't intend on being alone with these two?!"

"That is exactly what I intend," the woman said.

"But—"

"I said I'm speaking to them alone." Narrowed brown eyes glared out from between the bandages wrapped around her face. The man shuffled, and then, with great reluctance, he backed down. The woman nodded. "Good. Now come on, you two. Let's talk."

Left with no other option, Caspian and Elincia followed the woman whose name they had yet to learn.

Chapter 4

The hut that he and Elincia were led into was larger than he had expected. It seemed they had built this hut over a large hole in the ground, or perhaps they had dug out the hole before building the hut.

A ladder led deeper into the hut, which expanded into an underground chamber that was far larger than the tiny building that stood over it. The walls were packed with wooden posts to support the roof and keep the chamber from collapsing.

While the interior was spacious, about forty square meters in total, it didn't have much in the way of furnishings. There were no chairs, no beds, just a single table and several sleeping mats. Even then, the table was old and looked ready to fall apart, and the sleeping mats were threadbare and worn. It was clear that these people had been living in squalor.

"Sit down," the woman said. She glanced at Caspian as he was about to touch his sword. "Relax. I have no intention of trying to kill you two. I wouldn't have bothered saving you if that was the case."

Left with little choice, Caspian and Elincia sat down on the floor. From his position, he watched as the woman undid the bandages around her head. Long locks of grayish blonde hair fell about her aged face, which had numerous wrinkles around the mouth and eyes, crow's feet. She was much older than Caspian had imagined her to be. Not many people her age could fight like she had.

"You mentioned that you wanted to talk to us," Caspian prodded.

"That's right," the woman said, sitting down with a plop. "I wanted to know what a pair of highly capable people like yourselves are doing all the way out here."

Caspian raised an eyebrow. "Is that so? Well, I'd like to know what a group of suspiciously cloaked individuals are doing in a forest filled with undead?"

"You're a mouthy brat, ain't ya?" the woman said. She grinned when Caspian glared at her. "It should be obvious what we're doing here. A lot of people come by this way, since Exiguus is one of the stopover points to reach Helheim. We've been doing all we can to stop them from passing through."

"Because of the undead?" Elincia asked.

The woman nodded. "That's right. Now I believe it's your turn. What are you two doing coming up this way?"

"We're here to discover the source of the undead and exterminate it," Caspian said. "Several reports have made it to Casadinia stating that a necromancer has taken up residence in Parumé and—"

"A necromancer?" The woman laughed as if he'd just said something extraordinarily stupid. "You think a measly necromancer could be the cause of all this? Don't make me laugh!"

While Caspian scowled at the woman, Elincia asked, "if it's not a necromancer, then what is it?"

"A lich king," the woman answered.

Caspian's breath caught in his throat.

Lich kings were exceedingly powerful monsters. No one knew what they were, exactly, though many rumors and theories had been tossed about. The first recorded sighting of a lich king was 1,200 years ago, before humanity had cast off their elven shackles. Aside from being incredibly rare, lich kings were well-known for being physically imposing, frighteningly intelligent, and also, they had the most powerful necromantic abilities among all creatures that could use necromancy.

The first record of a lich king appearing was a story written by a human slave, documenting how, one day, a creature of unknown origins had raised an army of nearly 60,000 undead and started a war with the elves. It had been defeated. However, the death toll had been catastrophic, and since the humans had been used as cannon fodder during that war, they were the ones who suffered the most casualties. After the war, the elves had given that creature the name lich king.

"Caspian…" Elincia muttered as she looked over at him, her slender eyebrows creasing in concern.

"H-how long has this lich king been here?" Caspian asked, his voice shaky.

"That we don't know." The woman crossed her arms and glared at nothing, almost like she was looking through them instead of at them. "We don't have any idea how long the lich king has been living in these parts. What we do know is that one day, a number of undead attacked Exiguus, killing almost everyone there. Myself and the people with me are the only survivors who managed to escape."

"Do you know where the lich king has taken up residence?" Caspian continued questioning.

"Hold on." The woman raised her hand to forestall any more questions. "You've asked a lot of questions. Now it's my turn. You. Girl." She pointed at Elincia. "You're an elf, aren't you? What's an elf doing with a human? And how can you summon spirits like you did?"

Caspian didn't think this woman's question was appropriate considering the situation, but he also knew they didn't have any choice but to answer. They were in dire straits. Not considering the undead, they were also trapped inside of a hut with people who or may not respond to them with hostility.

Caspian was strong, and Elincia could summon a spirit should the need arise. Even so, it would be better to avoid a confrontation if possible.

"I might be an elf, but I'm also a sorceress," Elincia said.

"A elf and a sorceress, eh? Now I've heard everything." The woman chuckled, her throaty laughter making Caspian twitch. "And? What about that summoning ability? I don't know much about magic, but I know that elves shouldn't be able to summon spirits."

"It's… I'm not sure why I can summon spirits," Elincia admitted. "It's something that I've been able to do since I was little, but I have no idea why or even how it happened."

"Hmm…" The woman hummed, leaned back, and then clicked her tongue. "It doesn't seem like you're lying, so I guess I'll trust ya. Not like we have much choice. Even so, don't do anything that will make you lose that trust, got it?"

"Um, I understand."

"Good." The woman stood up. "Now, then, you two wait here."

The woman walked past them. Caspian turned his head to follow her. She stopped upon reaching the ladder and, turning around, she said, "That's right. I forgot to introduce myself, didn't I? My name is Jessie Falon. I'd say it's nice to meet you, but given our grim circumstances, I'm not really sure 'nice' is a word I can use right now."

"Considering our first meeting, I don't think saying 'nice to meet you' would be appropriate anyway," Caspian shot back.

"Heh, you're a funny guy," Jessie said, and then she was gone, the sound of her climbing up the ladder echoing down to them.

"What should we do now?" asked Elincia.

"There's not much that we can do." Caspian leaned back, using his arms for support, and stared at the dirt ceiling. "All we can do now is wait around and do our best to acquire more information. We'll make our decision then." He sighed. "I hope we don't have to wait long."

***

Jessie had called everyone inside and told them that he and Elincia would be staying with them for a while. She never specified when they would leave, and Caspian wasn't sure how long he wanted to stay. While a few people had moaned and complained about this, no one had actually contested Jessie's decision, making it clear that she was their undisputed leader.

The group had dinner that night. It wasn't anything special, just some rabbit stew, but Caspian had been so hungry that he'd barely tasted what he put in his mouth. He hadn't really thought about it, but after fighting against this group of people, fighting against the undead, and then running for so long without food, he was famished.

After dinner, Jessie had gathered everyone around the table. Caspian and Elincia stood off to the side, further away from everyone else, but close enough that everyone could see them. Elincia received some pretty nasty looks. Since Jessie already knew she was an elf, they had decided it was pointless to hide her ears. Fortunately, no one said anything to her.

"It seems these two were sent here by the Sorceress Council to investigate and exterminate the source creating the undead," Jessie told everyone.

"How can that be?" asked one of the men, an older man with a handlebar mustache and a bald head.

"Yeah, she's an elf," a younger boy with a head full of bushy hair and brown eyes said. "How can an elf be a sorceress?"

"I don't know how she became a sorceress, but you all saw what she did, how she summoned that spirit." Jessie spread her arms wide, as if the say, *"there you have it."*

"That doesn't mean anything. For all we know, she could be a spy for Fas Sheras."

The one who accused Elincia of being a spy had a worn face that made him look a decade older than he probably was. His reddish-brown hair was in complete disarray, made even more messy by how he periodically ran his hands through it. He was muscular, possessing the kind of muscles gained through hard labor instead of training. His clothing, a simple brown shirt that stretched tight across his pectorals and broad shoulders and brown carpenter pants, made Caspian think of a blacksmith or a woodworker. Steel gray eyes glared at Elincia with distrust.

"And what reason would the elves have to spy on the Sorceress Council, James?" asked Jessie.

"Clearly so they can get revenge on us humans for winning our freedom from them," the one called James said.

"You're telling me that you think Sylvia de Floresca, the one who fought against the elves and beat them, would let an elven spy into her ranks?" Jessie inquired.

"Maybe she doesn't know," James shot back.

"Lady Sylvia is the one who rescued me." Elincia stepped forward before anyone else could say anything. "After my family was attacked by a rebellious faction and I was forced to flee from my home, it was Lady Sylvia who took me into her home and gave me a purpose. I'm only alive now because of her. I don't care if you don't trust me. You're free to say whatever you want about me, but I won't listen to you slander her."

Caspian wouldn't say he was surprised when Elincia glared at the man, James, but he couldn't deny that it was a little shocking. Elincia had never really glared at anyone, to the best of his knowledge. She always spoke with a polite, well-mannered, and somewhat shy demeanor. She never raised her voice. She never got upset. At the same time, Sylvia was important to her. Even if they were sometimes at odds thanks to what happened during the tournament, it didn't change how Sylvia had taken her in when she had nowhere to go.

It wasn't known whether James sensed that, or if he was just frightened of elves. Either way, he stumbled backwards at Elincia's glare, which had enough fire to melt steel.

"We're not going to question your loyalty," Jessie said, stepping between the two. "Though you have to understand why we're so wary of you."

"No, I don't understand." Frowning at everyone, Elincia seemed more irritated than Caspian had seen her, save for a few times. "The war between humans and elves ended over one thousand years ago, and there hasn't been a single war since. Outside of about two dozen incidents that were perpetrated by elves who had been exiled, there's been no hostilities between us. So no, I don't understand why you're so wary of me. I don't get it at all."

She's frustrated. She's been trying so hard to make people accept her. She's made such great strides towards gaining that acceptance, but all that stopped the moment she was outed as an elf. It must seem like all of her hard work has gone to waste, like everything she did for the people who now revile her was pointless. I can't even begin to imagine how frustrated she is.

For six months Elincia had worked for the people, had met everyone with a smile, but now that they knew she was an elf, a good deal of those people distrusted her. Smiles had turned into glares. Acceptance had turned into suspicion. Even though some people had accepted her, it didn't change how the majority now glanced at her as though she would stab them in their sleep.

Sometimes, I wonder if humans and elves will ever come to understand one another.

"I… see," Jessie said at last. "You must have gone through a lot to get where you are. I'm sorry we're so wary of you. It's not easy overcoming centuries of fear. My parents, and my parents' parents, they always told us stories about how evil and frightening elves are. I guess it's become so ingrained in us that we've become used to fearing elves without reason."

Elincia didn't say anything. When Caspian looked in her direction, he noticed the way she was biting her lower lip. It was the expression she often wore when she was struggling with something.

Back when they were younger, every time she became frustrated by their homework, or when she was having trouble solving a puzzle, she would make that face. Caspian had always thought she looked unbearably cute when she did it.

Stepping forward, Caspian put a hand on Elincia's lower back. He didn't speak through their bond. Instead, he flooded her with his feelings, the feelings that he had for her, his desire to make her happy, to see her smile. Everything.

Her spine straightened as though it was being snapped back into place, and her cheeks suddenly took on a darkened hue. She blinked several times. Then she licked her lips as if they were dried out. She looked at him, a silent question in her eyes, but he just smiled before turning his attention to the people present.

"Regardless of your feelings about elves, Elincia and I are only here to do a job," Caspian said. "We were told that Parumé, a village that had once been destroyed, was now home to a necromancer. I'm assuming we received misinformation, or rather, no one realized we would be up against a lich king. However, it doesn't change our task. Elincia and I are going to Parumé to destroy the lich king before it becomes an even bigger problem."

"You must be crazy," James spoke into the silence. The sneer on his dirt-smudged face emphasized his words. "There's no way two people can beat a lich king, even if one of you is an elf who can summon spirits."

"I don't want to agree with him, but James has a point," Jessie said. "There's an entire army of undead between you and the lich king. You'll never get close to that monster with just the two of you."

What he and Elincia planned to do, what they had been tasked to do, probably sounded insane to most people. Lich kings were powerful. Several sorceresses had even been killed when one of them appeared a few hundred years ago. The only person who had even managed to kill a lich king by herself was none other than Sylvia.

It was one of the parts of history that Arcadia's Knight Academy had in their textbooks. The history text stated that Sylvia and her knight of the time, a man named Acario, had fought against a lich king on the Athorian plains south of Attoré. The battle had lasted for seven days and nights. Then, on the eighth day as the sun was rising, Sylvia had summoned Odin and destroyed the lich king using an Aria with the most verses in recorded history.

No one knew how many verses her chant had been. Sylvia never spoke of her accomplishments. Some of the history teachers had theorized that the Aria had taken an entire day to complete. In the end, all they had was over exaggerated speculation.

"We could send a message back to Sylvia, asking her to send us reinforcements," Caspian said. "But there's no telling how long it would take for her to get the letter, much less send reinforcements, and who knows what could happen during that time."

"So going up against a lich king on your own is better?" asked Jessie. "Sounds like a dumb way to get yourself killed."

"And what about you?" Caspian, more than willing to return fire, said. "Your village has become overrun with undead, but you're still staying around on the outskirts. How is that any better?"

Jessie glared hard at Caspian, who was more than willing to return it. He could practically see the sparks sizzling between them, and even though he could see her point, Caspian didn't want to admit it.

This wasn't a matter of bravado. No one knew how lich kings worked. They were a complete mystery. If left alone, this one could easily begin destroying other villages, turning more villagers into undead, and expanding its army. If that happened, there might be another war between humans and a lich king.

He couldn't back down.

"Caspian," Elincia said softly. "I agree with Jessie. It might be better to send out a message asking for aid and wait for a response before making any moves."

Had anyone else said that, he would have argued with them. This was Elincia, however, and she was his sorceress. Even if he had been inclined to argue, which he wasn't, he was duty bound to follow her decision, whatever that decision might be.

"How would we get a message out?" he asked. "Our horse is gone."

"We actually reclaimed your horse the other day," Jessie said. "He's at one of our other hideouts. It's closer to the forest entrance."

"Given the situation, we can't leave even if we wanted to. There's still too much we don't know," Caspian said. "We need to gather as much information as we can about this situation."

"Then you can write the letter and one of my boys will travel to

Axium and have it delivered," Jessie countered. "Then you can do whatever information gathering you want while you wait. That said, if you do plan on exploring the region, I'll have to ask you not to do anything stupid."

"Caspian…" Elincia muttered.

"All right. You win." Caspian sighed. He glanced at Elincia out of the corner of his eyes. Big blue eyes stared back at him. "I could never win when you give me such an imploring look."

"Then it's settled." Jessie clapped her hands together. "Stay here for tonight. Tomorrow morning, one of my boys will go off with your letter and make sure it's been delivered safely."

There appeared to be nothing more that needed to be said. Everyone broke off into groups. Some people went outside, presumably to stand watch, while others simply chose a spot and sat down. James gave him and Elincia one more glare before stomping off somewhere. Meanwhile, Jessie walked over to them.

"Since you mentioned wanting to gather information, I'm guessing you have a plan?" she prodded.

Elincia looked at Caspian, who noticed the question in her eyes, causing him to sigh and cross his arms. "While one of your people heads out to deliver the letter, I plan on going around to the other villages in this area. I need to see how many have become nests of undead. I need to know how far the lich king's reach has extended. I'd also like to find out if you guys are the only survivors."

"I suppose that's a sound enough plan for now," Jessie agreed. "In that case, I would suggest you two get some rest. If you plan to start investigating immediately, you'll want to be well-rested."

"Yes, I suppose so."

"Come on." Jessie gestured for him and Elincia to follow her. "I'll lend you two a blanket to sleep on. I've only got one, though, so you'll have to share. That's not a problem, is it?"

Caspian and Elincia looked at each other. Then they blushed and looked away. Jessie laughed at them, which made his lips twist into a scowl, even as his face turned another shade of red.

He somehow understood that he was never going to live this

moment down.

Chapter 5

Elincia wrote a letter to the Sorceress Council the previous night with a request for them to send another sorceress. Since Sylvia had no knowledge of the real enemy, Elincia also made sure to include the information that they were up against a lich king. Barring everything else, should that information come to light, Sylvia was sure to send someone to back them up—that was their hope.

Jessie sent one of her "boys" off to deliver the letter. It had been a younger man in his early or mid-twenties. Caspian couldn't remember his name, though he believed it started with a B. Either way, the young man had taken off to the other hideout, where the horse that he and Elincia had been using before they were attacked was hidden.

After eating a sparse breakfast, Caspian prepared himself both physically and mentally for their upcoming investigation. He needed to be ready for anything. He also needed to plot out a route to take. Since there was no telling how far the lich king's influence had expanded into other parts of Arcadia, Caspian wanted to make sure nothing would surprise him.

The room was mostly dark. However, there were several spirit crystal lamps arrayed around the room. One of them sat on the table, which Caspian stood before, hands resting on the wooden surface, fingers splayed. Before him was a map of Terraria.

Terraria was shaped like a giant, misshapen oval. Several inlets, peninsulas, and capes destroyed any form of symmetry. Arcadia sat in the center of this oval. To north lay Helheim; Takama no Hara sat east of Arcadia, while Elysium was west, and Moksha was in the south. Between each of these four nations, either a forest, inlet sea, or a desert separated them.

"Caspian?" Elincia came up to him from behind, stopping on his left. She looked down at the map that was spread across the table.

"Ele," he greeted. "I didn't think you'd wake up so early. Wouldn't you like to sleep in a bit more? We have time."

Elincia shook her head. "No, I've rested enough. What are you doing?"

"I'm trying to determine which routes we should take during our investigation," Caspian replied. Putting his index finger on the map, he drew a curving line along it as though pointing out the trail they would follow. "We should first visit Exiguus. Jessie said all of the people there have been turned into undead, but it'll make a good starting point. Then I was thinking we'd journey northwest. There are several small villages along the way that are about the same size as Exiguus." He moved his finger again, traveling inward this time. "Afterward, we'll travel northeast. Then we'll traverse back south, but we'll go further east to figure out how far the lich king's reach has extended."

"What about Parumé?" asked Elincia.

"Parumé is right here." Caspian pointed to a spot on the very edge of Arcadia. "It borders the Andolian Mountain Range, beyond which is said to lie a barren wasteland. There's a ravine that travels through the mountain range. We have no knowledge of what's beyond this mountain, so all we have are rumors and hearsay. That's probably where the lich king came from."

The Andolian Mountain Range extended for several hundred kilometers north and south. According to the map, it then curled inward on either side, thereby cutting the wasteland, which was known as the Dead Tundra, from both Helheim and Takama no Hara. No one had ever traveled into the Dead Tundra and returned, so they didn't know what lay beyond. That was why that section of the map had been left blank.

"How long will it take to travel this distance?" asked Elincia.

"If we walk the entire distance and don't run into any trouble, it will take about two weeks," Caspian said. "Of course, it'll take around two weeks for that letter to reach Sylvia, provided there are no mishaps, so we should make it back in time for whoever they send to reinforce us." He paused as Elincia bit her lower lip. "Are you worried?"

"A little," she confessed, though she was quick to say, "ah! But, it's not that I don't think you're incapable of protecting me. I know how strong you are. I'm just worried about what will happen if we're overrun with undead, or if I end up overusing my magic. If I were to run out of mana when we're in danger, I'd be practically useless."

It was the continual problem of being an elven sorceress. Mana consumption.

Caspian wondered if there was some way around this particular issue. He knew that Elincia used less mana to do partial summonings, but that still consumed several times more mana than chanting an Aria did. The problem was that Elincia couldn't chant Aria's. Her magic simply didn't work that way.

Thinking about it, this actually placed a larger burden on him than if Elincia was a normal sorceress. Since she needed to be careful, lest she run out of mana, she couldn't use too much summoning magic. He would have to protect her, and he wouldn't have the benefit of her being able to dish out spells nonstop like he would if she'd been a regular sorceress. That was something he'd have to keep in mind going into this.

"We'll just have to be careful," he said at last. "If things get too dangerous, we'll retreat to a safer distance. Undead can't stray too far from the lich king that created them. I don't know the range, since there's never been a clear answer, but depending on the power of the lich king, it can supposedly be anywhere from a few dozen to one hundred kilometers. That might even be why the lich king hasn't expanded further than Exiguus."

This was just a guess based on arbitrary numbers with no real foundation. There wasn't enough information about lich kings to judge how accurate these numbers were, but it would explain why the lich king had remained in this area.

Lich kings were intelligent. It likely knew that the Sorceress Council would dispose of it before its plans were complete if it extended its reach further than this, so it remained in Parumé, gathering forces a little at time to expand its powerbase. Caspian guessed that it was trying to build up its forces by turning citizens of the smaller villages around this area into undead before making an attempt on the larger cities like Axium.

"You think so?" Elincia asked.

Caspian shrugged. "Maybe. There's no way to know for sure. It's just a theory."

Their itinerary, which they changed several times to more efficiently traverse the area within a limited timeframe, was eventually completed.

During that time, numerous people came and went. Many of them stared at him and Elincia, but no one came up and spoke with them. Caspian guessed they were not comfortable being close to an elf. That would explain why Jessie had them sleep far away from everyone else last night.

Leading Elincia outside, Caspian needed to blink several times as sunlight struck him in the face. After being cooped up inside of that dark room for so long, having the sun, which seemed to be shining abnormally brightly that day, glaring into his eyes hurt.

"Looks like you two are ready to head out," Jessie said as she walked up to them. Hands on her hips, clad in a dark cloak, the woman looked like an old bandit crow who was well past her prime.

"My boys went back to your carriage and grabbed your items. You should look through them and decide what you want to bring before leaving. You should also pack some food with you. There's no telling whether or not you'll find anything edible during your travels."

"We'll do that," Caspian said. "Thanks."

Jessie shrugged. "Considering you two are here to get rid of that lich king, this is the least I can do. I still think your quest is foolish, but I'm grateful all the same."

Farewells were said, though only to Jessie, and the sorceress/knight pair were soon on their way.

The day was just beginning as Caspian and Elincia set out on their journey.

***

Their first stop was Exiguus. They were fortunate not to run into any undead. Where before there had been hundreds of undead chasing after them, now there were none.

Caspian didn't know if this meant the undead couldn't come out during the day, or if there was a limit to the lich king's control. Perhaps it could only command a few undead at a time, or maybe it had sent them all elsewhere. There wasn't any way to know for sure. Caspian supposed they should just be grateful.

"This place is completely empty," Elincia muttered as they wandered down a small dirt road. It was the only road in this village.

Buildings lined either side of the road. They weren't large. They were actually rather small. Each building had a basic square design, was made from wood, and had a slanted roof. Looking into the windows as he shifted the pack slung around his shoulder, Caspian could see that even the interiors were empty—at least from where he was looking.

"It's kind of creepy, isn't it?" Caspian whispered, though he had no idea why he was whispering. Something about this place made him feel like he'd be damning them if he spoke louder.

"Yeah… it is," Elincia agreed.

There weren't many buildings. Caspian counted twenty

buildings in total, and most of them appeared to be houses, though they passed one that, judging from the forging equipment, was a blacksmith's workshop. A couple of stands were also sitting on the roadside in front of the houses. The people who lived in those houses must have been vendors. He could picture how this place must looked during the day, before the undead had attacked it. It was easy to imagine men and women setting up their shops, greeting everyone who came by because everyone knew everyone else. He could almost see the smiles on imaginary faces as he walked past the empty stalls and buildings.

Thinking about how such a peaceful village had been wiped out was depressing.

What Caspian guessed was the mayor's house stood at the road's end, still miniscule compared to what he was used to, but larger than any other building there. With two stories, a lot more space, and several decorations lining the outside such as basic columns, it was the most extravagant structure present.

The front entrance was marked by a small staircase that ascended into a shaded porch. They creaked only slightly when he and Elincia walked up them. Doric columns kept the roof from collapsing, and the white door seemed in perfect working order.

Caspian walked up to the front door, a basic contraption made of wood, with a wooden frame and an iron handle. He didn't knock. If this place really was a dead town, then there wouldn't be anyone coming to greet them, so he just turned the handle.

It was unlocked.

The door creaked as Caspian opened it, a low groaning that made him wince. It sounded out several decibels louder than it should have in the silent town. As he stepped into the building, he moved aside so that Elincia could follow him, and glanced at the interior.

It wasn't what he would call opulent. That said, the entrance hall was decently spacious, spanning what Caspian had to guess was ten square meters. Carpet shifted underneath their feet as they walked further into the room. There weren't any decorations, no furniture or paintings, not even a single statue.

Living in a city really was different than living in a small village.

"What are we looking for, exactly?" asked Elincia.

"I'm not sure." Caspian shrugged. "I wouldn't say we're looking for something specific so much as getting a feel for the town. We can check out some of the smaller buildings before we leave for the next one."

Elincia nodded, and together, they went through a door located on the far side, which led into a narrow hallway. The wooden floorboards creaked as they walked. Because there were no windows and the spirit crystal lamps didn't seem to be working, the hallway was dark, though he and Elincia could see just fine. Nothing looked out of place. Once again, Caspian noticed there were no decorations of any sort.

One by one, they checked each room. The first floor had four rooms in total. One of them was a guest room, but there was also a kitchen, a dining room, and a lounge with a small library. It was the library that Caspian and Elincia ended up spending the most time in.

"There isn't a wide selection, but the mayor has very good taste in books," Elincia said as she read the titles from the spine. "I've read quite a few of these."

"It looks like a lot of them are fiction titles," Caspian murmured as he glanced through the selection.

The library wasn't that big. It was, at most, the same size as the entrance hall, and it only had four bookshelves worth of books. Compared to the library inside of Dorehan Tower, this wasn't even worthy of being called a library. Sylvia's personal library was also larger. Outside of the bookshelves, there was a small sitting area with a wooden table surrounded by several cushioned chairs.

Just like Caspian had said, most of the books were fiction, which Elincia loved to read. Caspian was more of a non-fiction reader. He preferred reading books that were informative as opposed to ones that told fictional stories and fairy tales. If anything, Caspian would much rather watch Elincia as she read. Seeing the way her face lit up when she was reading always brightened his day.

Caspian opened his mouth to suggest they leave the library and search the second floor—

A loud crash from somewhere outside made his throat close up, the words sticking as if they'd been glued to the inside of his mouth.

"What was that?" asked Elincia.

Caspian didn't answer with words. He rushed toward the door as more crashing echoed all around them, followed by the pounding of feet. As he opened the door, Caspian received the shock of his life when, without warning, several hands tried to grab him. Undead hands. Rotting flesh that attempted to claw at his face.

Leaping back, Caspian pulled his sword free of its sheath and swung. "Halkaista!" His shout was followed by the blade arcing through the air, slicing the undead straight down the middle.

This offered little reprieve. Not even a second passed before more undead came in through the door, moving with lumbering, awkward steps. Caspian didn't waste any time in dispatching him. He cleaved through them with his blade and magic, always making sure to aim for their heads. Yet no matter how many he killed, more seemed to come.

"Caspian!" At the sound of his name being called, Caspian leapt off to the side. Standing behind him, Elincia held out her hand, and shouted, "Thor! Please help me!"

Appearing in a swirling vortex of crackling energy, a bolt of lightning shot out from the aether and slammed into the undead that were pouring through the door.

Caspian leapt backward and covered his face with his hands as the building shook. Wood chips flew everywhere as the lightning bolt blasted the door and much of the wall apart. It wasn't just the building that received damage. All of the undead were destroyed, decimated. What few undead had not been turned into steaming chunks of flesh were lying on the ground, twitching sporadically as though undergoing muscle spasms. All of them were dead… er. They were no longer moving, and that was what mattered.

It took Caspian a full second to appreciate the power of

Elincia's—Thor's—attack. There was no way he could have done so much damage, and it would have required at least a six or seven verse Aria for a sorceress to accomplish the same thing. He shook himself out of his stupor, though, realizing that they couldn't afford to remain in one place.

"Let's go, Ele!"

"Right!"

Running through the hole in the wall, Caspian and Elincia burst into the entrance hall. Nearly a dozen undead were standing around or clambering back to their feet, having been sent sprawling by the bolt of lightning's aftershock. All of them turned toward him and Elincia, however, and began to stumble after them.

Because he didn't want Elincia wasting her mana on these small fry, Caspian leapt forward, sword in hand. With a shout of, "halkaista!" he sliced through an undead, cleaving its torso from its legs. Spinning around, he shouted again and swung his sword in a diagonal slashing attack that bisected another undead from left hip to right shoulder.

"Get to the stairs!" he shouted at Elincia before throwing himself at another undead. He raised his sword and prepared to bring it down.

He hesitated.

The one before him was a child. It was a little girl. She couldn't have been more than six or seven years old. Her skin had the same sickly pallor as every other undead, her eyes were the same milky white orbs found on corpses, and rotting flesh sloughed off her body. Even the muscles in her jaw were visible thanks to the large chunk of missing skin along her face.

She wasn't alive. She wasn't alive she wasn't alive she was dead. She was an undead. Whatever she had once been didn't matter anymore.

Caspian still hesitated.

"Caspian!" Elincia shouted from the stares.

The little girl lunged.

She was cut down.

Caspian's eyes stung as he swung his blade down, slicing through the air hard enough to produce a loud whistling sound. Gravity helped ensure that his sword cut through the little girl's skull. After it passed through her, blood spraying everywhere as her face split open, she dropped to the ground with a boneless tumble.

Gritting his teeth, Caspian fought against the tears as he cut down two more undead, and then ran up the stairs to join Elincia.

"Thor!" Elincia called out again as Caspian reached the second floor.

A bolt of lightning slammed into the staircase. Several undead that had been trying to reach them were pulverized, their bodies fried to the point that they disintegrated. A wave of heat followed by an even more intense electric current washed over him and Elincia, making them both yelp as blue lightning skittered across their bodies, not harming them, but not at all pleasant to feel. Multiple undead were thrown backwards, away from the now decimated staircase.

"This is the only way to reach the second floor," Elincia said. "We should be safe for now." When Caspian didn't respond, she turned to him. "Are you okay?"

Caspian shook his head. "No, I'm not… but now isn't the time to get emotional. We have to escape from this place."

"How are we going to do that?"

"Follow me."

Caspian led Elincia to the nearest window, opened it, and stuck his head outside. Exiguus was overrun. Undead filled the streets, filling what appeared to be every nook, cranny, and crevice. There were so many of them—too many. This had to be more than just the people of Exiguus. He suspected that most of these undead belonged to another village, maybe even several.

How did they all get here? Did the lich king send them? How would he even know we're here?

Looking around, Caspian spotted what he was searching for. Several vines crawled up the wall. They were thick and seemed sturdy enough to climb.

"Caspian? What are you doing?" asked Elincia as he sat on the window sill, practically hanging off it.

"Getting to the roof," he answered.

Reaching out with a hand, Caspian grasped the nearest vine and hauled himself out of the window. The vines creaked. Caspian felt his stomach drop as he almost fell when the vines loosened. They held, fortunately, and Caspian quickly climbed up as Elincia stuck her head out of the window to watch him.

He climbed onto the roof. Standing up, Caspian pulled the pack that he had been carrying on his back off and set it on the ground. It took him a moment of searching through it to find what he was looking for. Then he pulled out a long rope and, after trying one end around his torso, he stood at the lip of the roof and dangled the other end in front of the window.

"Grab hold of the rope," he commanded. "I'll use it to pull you up."

A moment after he dropped the rope, a weight suddenly appearing on the other end nearly made him stumble forward. Elincia dangled on the end of the rope. Her eyes were wide, and she was clutching the rope as though her life depended on it. Caspian bent his knees and braced himself. Then, with a grunt of effort and a strain of his muscles, he slowly pulled on the rope until Elincia was close enough for him to grab her hands and pull her up.

"Okay. We're on the roof," Elincia said, looking a little shaken. "Now what?"

Caspian looked at the village. More specifically, he looked at the undead littering the village. All of them had congregated around the building they were standing on. He couldn't see any further out, though he didn't discount the possibility that there were more undead waiting beyond the trees.

"We're going to jump from roof to roof until we're out of the village," Caspian replied. "The distance between this roof and the next one is about twenty meters or so. I can make the jump easily." He knelt down in front of Elincia. "Here, climb onto my back. It'll be easier for me to jump if I carry you piggyback."

It was a testament to their bond that Elincia didn't question him;

she climbed onto his back without a second's hesitation. Caspian placed his hands underneath her thighs as he stood up. Her supple muscles twitched beneath his fingers, and her arms wrapped tightly around his neck.

Caspian took several steps back.

For this, he would need a running start.

He took a deep breath, held it, and then, like a cannonball as it burst out of a cannon, he rushed forward. As he reached the edge of the roof, he shouted, "springen!" and leapt.

Wind rushed around him as he soared through the sky. His eyes stung, but he kept them open, watching as the other roof came ever closer. Ten meters. Five Meters. One.

His feet hit the roof. The wood splintered underneath them, and Caspian realized from the way it groaned that it was going to break soon. He rushed toward the other side, leapt, and landed on the next roof, and then the next one, and the next one, until, eventually, there were no more buildings to jump to.

He jumped off the last roof.

Caspian's impact with the ground sent lances of agony up and down his legs. It felt like one of his shins had splintered under the combined weight of him and Elincia, made worse by the fact that he hadn't been able to turn his leap into a roll to help absorb the impact. Gnashing his teeth together, he pushed himself into a quick trot, ignoring the pain, and ran into the trees.

There was no telling how far he had run, for Caspian ran without direction. It didn't matter where he ran to. Getting as far from that village as he possibly could was the only thing that mattered.

Day turned to night and still Caspian ran. Elincia clung to his neck as trees blurred through his field of vision. He didn't know how long he had kept up this pace, but eventually, his legs began to tire, and his body to ache. The pain in his knees nearly made him faceplant into the earth several times. After traveling as far as he could, he slowly stopped running and sank to the ground.

"Ha… ha…" Caspian's ragged gasps accompanied the rapid

beating of his own heart. "I think… we've gotten… far enough… away…"

"Um," Elincia responded mutely, seemingly unable to say anything.

"We should be safe," Caspian repeated to himself. "We should…"

The more time that passed as he sat there, on his knees, the more overwhelming the feelings inside of him became. His stomach twisted itself into knots. He felt sick, like he wanted to vomit all over the forest floor. Beyond the feeling of being sick was a deep, aching sadness, a sorrow that threatened to swallow him up as though it was a black hole, an inescapable void.

"Caspian…?"

"I had to kill a little girl," Caspian whispered. "She couldn't have been older than Tiffania, and I killed her. Ele, I—"

"You didn't!" Elincia cut him off. She slid off his back and moved around until she was in front of him. A pair of delicate hands cupped his cheek and raised his face, forcing him to look into the emerald eyes of Elincia. "You didn't kill her, Caspian. She was already… she was gone long before we even arrived. You know that. All… all you did was make sure her body could no longer be desecrated by the lich king. You didn't do anything wrong."

"Is that so?" His eyes stung as something warm and wet trailed down his face. "Then why do I… feel so awful? Why does my chest hurt like this? Why do I feel like I've committed an unforgivable sin?"

Elincia shook her head. "I can't answer that. If our positions had been reversed, I'd probably be feeling the same way you do." In spite of the situation, or perhaps because of it, Elincia gave him a reassuring smile. "But you know, if it had been me who killed that little girl, you would be saying the same thing that I am right now, right?"

"P-probably." Caspian took a shaky, halting breath as, much like a machine that was out of spirit crystals, all of the strength fled from his body, and he fell face first against Elincia's chest. "I'm sorry… do you mind if I stay like this for a while?"

Elincia's answer was to wrap her arms around his head. "Of course you can. Stay like this for as long as you need."

"Thank you, Ele, and…"

"I love you," the words sprang from his mind, for his mouth was too tired to say them.

"I know." Her response. *"I love you, too."*

Alone together in the forest, Caspian clung to Elincia as though she were his only lifeline.

Chapter 6

Caspian and Elincia continued their journey the next day. They had been too exhausted to travel the night before, and so they'd slept wrapped up in each other's arms against a tree. Since they only had one blanket, they'd needed to share it, and it was better sleeping together because it let them share body heat during the cold night.

That had been their excuse, at least.

The next morning, Elincia had summoned Eir to heal Caspian's leg, which had been broken from leaping off that last building and onto the ground. She would have done so the previous night, but her mana had been exhausted. After his leg was healed, they set off.

Their journey took them out of the forest that surrounded Exiguus and into the rural plains of Ruudon. As he and Elincia traveled along a dirt road, he looked to his left, at the rustling wheat fields as a cool breeze blew through them. High overhead, storm clouds gathered in the distance.

"Looks like it'll rain sometime today," Caspian said.

While his communion with nature was not at the level of a full-blooded elf, he still had enough sense to be capable of predicting the weather—not that one needed to be an elf to know it would rain. The gathering storm clouds were heading this way.

"Seems that way," Elincia agreed. "We should probably hurry to the next town. How far away is it?"

"Our next destination is Flos. It's supposed to be larger than most of the villages around here, but it's still pretty small. We should be there after a few more hours of walking."

"We've been walking for some time already."

"Yeah."

It was true. They had started walking early this morning, when the sun was just beginning to peak over the mountains in the east. Now the sun was high above their heads. It beat down on them with its radiance. Caspian thought they were fortunate that this area had such a cool breeze blowing through it, or they'd have probably suffered from heat stroke by now.

"Caspian?" Elincia said suddenly.

"Yes?"

"Do you…" she hesitated before plunging on. "Are you feeling okay today? After what happened yesterday, I'm worried about you."

Smiling at her concern, Caspian took Elincia's hand. "I'm fine. I know there was nothing more that I could have done. It rankles on me, and it hurts, but I understand that what happened wasn't something that could be helped." He clenched his left hand until it formed a tight fist, leather glove creaking. "If anything, the blame for what happened to that little girl lies at the lich king's feet. It's just another reason we need to defeat that monster."

They couldn't let atrocities like this happen anymore. Caspian didn't want to be forced to commit more brutal acts like what he had done to that little girl ever again.

"Hm." Elincia nodded. "We can't afford to let what happened to those people continue."

"Right."

As they traveled along the dirt road, which meandered in gentle patterns that curved left and right, Caspian thought about Exiguus, about the girl, and about the lich king who was the cause of all this. It was hard for him to believe that the lich king had gone uncontested for so long.

Then again, it hasn't been that long, has it? The letter that Sylvia received wasn't dated, but if it had been sent from Parumé, then it would've taken around a month to reach Casadinia. That's not a very long time, all things considered. Still...

Caspian was bothered by something. To the best of his knowledge, Parumé had never been rebuilt. From the time he'd been rescued to now, it should have remained a ruin.

Of course, it could have been rebuilt and he just never knew about it. It wasn't like he had thought about his old hometown much. It was actually something he had tried to forget. Caspian had done everything he could think of to bury the memories of his life in Parumé so deep in his mind that nothing could bring them back. At the same time...

That does beg the question of how long the lich king has been here. Did the lich king take up residence at my hometown that day ten years ago, or are these two events unrelated?

It was an answer that he wouldn't find out until he got to Parumé. However, he couldn't imagine these two events not being related.

"Caspian," Elincia said suddenly. "Someone is coming."

A glance at the road revealed that a carriage was traveling their way. From this distance, he could make out many of the finer detailers. The carriage wasn't being drawn by a horse, but by a land dragon, a horse-sized lizard that walked on two legs, with scaly green skin and bright yellow eyes. Behind the land dragon was the carriage. It was a plain flatbed carriage like the one they had been using before Jessie and her group had ambushed them. The person sitting on it was an older gentleman wearing a straw hat.

"You'd better hide your ears," Caspian said as he made sure his red headband also did an adequate job of hiding his slightly pointed ears.

While they weren't necessarily hiding her elf features anymore, it would be hard to hold a conversation if the person they were talking to was busy freaking out. They also couldn't afford to insight any panic.

"Right. Loki?"

The air thrummed with a tense hum. It was not a noise, but more like a vibration that suddenly filled the air and made Caspian's ears shake. Elincia's ears soon shrank, the points becoming rounded and more like a human's. Of course, it was really just a trick of the light, an illusion. If Caspian were to touch her ears, they would have still felt pointed.

Seconds after the illusion was cast, the carriage wheeled up alongside of them. The old man steering the land dragon looked down at the pair and grinned. "G'morning to ya. Great day, isn't it?"

"Yes," Elincia agreed with a smile that she probably didn't feel. "It's a very good day."

"Are you coming from Flos?" asked Caspian.

"Yep," the old man replied. "I just went over there to deliver my products. Barely stayed for a day before I had to leave again. The life of a farmer is never easy."

Because Ruudon was very rural, the people living there were often quite friendly. Areas that dealt in mostly farming had people who didn't really possess the same concept of time that city folks did. Since they weren't always rushing to work, they were willing to spend more time chatting with random strangers. This was also how farmers, merchants, and other travelers gained news of other areas.

"Have you noticed anything odd?" asked Elincia.

"Odd?" The old man blinked several times. "No, I don't reckon I have. Is something wrong?"

From those words, Caspian inferred that Flos had yet to be hit by the lich king. That meant its reach didn't extend this far out yet. This was good. On the other hand, there was no telling how long the city would remain untouched.

"Not this far out, it seems," Caspian replied, shaking his head. "There's no problem, but if you're traveling down this road, I'd recommend not going east."

"Why's that? Something bad happened?"

"We just came from Exiguus. It was filled with undead," Elincia said.

"W-what? Un—how?" The old man stumbled over his words, his tone shaking. His face had grown pale and his eyes wide.

"We're actually investigating the cause right now, and we're also warning everyone we meet to stay away from the forest," Caspian said.

"I see. You two… are a sorceress and her knight, aren't you?" the old man asked.

Nodding, Elincia said, "we are. We've been sent by the Sorceress Council to find out what's wrong and eliminate the problem."

"I see." Sighing, the old man slumped in his seat. "I'm relieved to hear that. Fortunately, I don't take the eastern road. My farm is southwest of here, so I won't be going near Exiguus."

"That's good," Caspian said.

"Take care." Elincia raised her hand in farewell.

As the old man drove off, Caspian and Elincia continued their journey to Flos. The village may be safe for the moment, but with a lich king on the loose, anything could happen. They needed to hurry that way and warn whoever was in charge.

Time was of the essence.

***

Flos was a village known for its myriad of flowers. Even from a distance, Caspian could distinguish Flos from the rest of the landscape simply from the cornucopia of colors. As they walked closer, the colors became a lot more distinct, revealing the reason why it had been nicknamed Flower Village.

None of the buildings were spared from the colorful blossoms; flowers ran along the walls, covered the roofs, and decorated numerous balconies. As they passed under an archway composed entirely of flowers, Caspian noticed that Flos really was a good deal larger than Exiguus. Several roads branched off from the main one. Although there were no paved roads, the cobblestone that made up much of the street lent it a rustic appeal that complemented all of the flora.

A lot of people were strolling through the village. Some appeared to have a destination in mind, but others seemed to simply be gossiping. A pair of ladies over there chatted about this and that. Two old men sat around a chess table and played a game whilst bickering. Caspian and Elincia moved out of the way as a group of children ran past them, laughing and cheering as they played some kind of game. Did they not have school today?

Like most small villages, this one had only a dozen or so shops, but it did have a lot of stands. They lined either side of the streets. Most were standard stands, just a table with a cloth tent over it, but a few were more modern-looking, like the crepe stand. Men and women stood behind their stalls, talking up their wares.

Most of them sold the standard fare: fruits and vegetables, clothing and jewelry. However, some of them sold arranged flowers, others sold flower bracelets, and still some sold flower headbands and rings and anklets.

"I'm beginning to notice a pattern here," Caspian said.

Elincia smiled. "Don't you think it's nice being in a place that's so peaceful?"

"I do." He smiled, though it vanished soon after when a soft sigh escaped his lips. He grabbed Elincia's hand and spoke telepathically. *"I also know that this village might not remain this way for long if we don't deal with the lich king soon."*

"Should we move on?"

"No. I think we should see the mayor and inform him about the situation. It's clear to me that no one knows what's happened to the villages west of here."

News traveled slowly in rural provinces. They had no system of communication set up, so it normally took months and even years to get news. That might also explain why no one knew about the lich king this far out. If the lich king had been staying in Parumé and hadn't made a move until recently, then no one would have known about what happened.

Elincia bit her lip for a moment, then slowly nodded. *"In which case, our duty is to inform the leader so he can create an appropriate plan in case the lich king sends its undead legion here."*

"Exactly."

Getting directions from one of the women they passed, Caspian and Elincia learned that the mayor's house was located on a large hill in the center of the city. They could even see it from where they stood. The hill was indeed large. Easily bigger than the surrounding buildings, all of which were one, two, or three-stories tall, the hill was characterized by the looping cobblestone road that traversed up it in a circle. On top of that hill was a small mansion.

Following the main road, Caspian and Elincia walked up and down several small hills, their hands clasped as the cobblestone path undulated and curved. There weren't any MAFTs in the village, not that Caspian could see. However, they did pass a couple of carriages. Some were being pulled by a horse, but most used land dragons.

This section of Ruudon was home to the largest land dragon population in Arcadia. Caspian didn't know where they were, but he knew that several dragon farms were located in this region.

They were large plots of open land. The people who owned this land bred land dragons to become a strong workforce. There was actually a Peacekeeper brigade known as the Dragon Riders stationed in Arcadia, and rumors abound that it was the land dragons in this region that they used. They were like a cavalry who used land dragons instead of horses.

It took a bit of time, but they soon reached the hill, which was a lot more imposing up close. The hill was so large that it cast shadows over him and Elincia. It was a lot more like a small mountain. Caspian couldn't even see the mansion sitting at the top.

"Well, shall we?" he asked.

Elincia responded, *"... Yes. Let's go."*

The road up the hill was clear of traffic. Not surprising. This mansion clearly belonged to a minor noble. While the mansion's size meant that whoever lived there was a low-ranking noble, they were still a noble. It was probably some stuffy old bastard living up there, sipping his wine from on high as he looked down at the plebs, all the while scheming up ways to raise his status.

There was a huge disparity between nobles and peasants; even the lowest ranking noble liked to lord his status over others. They were a narcissistic bunch. Case in point, Caspian only knew one noble who wasn't a complete douche.

"You really are pessimistic about nobles, aren't you?" asked Elincia.

Caspian shrugged. *"Of course. It's hard to trust nobles after everything they've done to me. They're filled with greedy people who would sooner stab you in the back than help you."*

"What about Christo?"

Caspian paused. *"Christo... is an exception."*

His words made Elincia giggle, though all this did was cause him to scowl and turn his head, the better to hide his blush.

They reached the top of the hill. With two stories and a good deal of width, the mansion did indeed look small—larger than anything else in Flos, but still smaller than most noble mansions. It also didn't have many decorations. There were no statues, columns, or anything else. Walking onto a stone porch, the two stopped in front of a door. Wood. Glossy finish. It, too, possessed few embellishments.

It seems the noble who lives here is very poor indeed.

Caspian knocked on the door, and then stepped back, waiting. They didn't have to wait long. A soft *click* signified someone unlocking the door, which opened a second later to reveal...

"Oh, my! I have guests!"

The woman who stood before them was... young. She didn't look any older than him and Elincia. Her auburn hair was styled into several ringlets that framed her pale face, which was marked by vivid blue eyes, a smattering of freckles, a button nose, and pink lips. Her outfit was pink and white, a dress of numerous frills and a puffy skirt that went down to her knees.

"I haven't seen you two before," she said, stepping back into the mansion and away from the door. The frills of her pink gown bounced as she moved, and the poufy skirt that flared out swished around her ankles. "Won't you please come in?"

"Uh… okay," Elincia said.

Being the sorceress, Elincia entered first, followed by Caspian who once more shifted into his role of a sorceress' knight. As they walked into the tiled room, the young woman shut the door behind them. She then walked to stand before them, her small figure looking even more tiny within the decently sized foyer.

Caspian absently realized that the inside looked larger than it truly was because there was no artwork, columns, or anything clogging the place. The only thing that decorated this room was the large variety of flowers that were sitting in vases of varying size and shape.

"Please, follow me," the woman said. "While we could talk here, I believe the courtyard is more suited to a discussion."

As the woman walked off, pink slipper shoes tapping against the tiles, Caspian and Elincia looked at each other. This was not what they had expected.

"I guess we follow her," he said.

"Right." Elincia nodded.

Elincia caught up to the young woman while Caspian hung a few paces back. As they walked past a staircase and into a hallway filled with red carpet, Elincia sought to ask the woman some questions.

"Excuse me, but do you mind if I ask who the lord of this house is? Will we get to see him soon?"

"The lord?" The young woman smiled as if Elincia had said something amusing. "There is no lord. You are currently looking at the lady of the house." Elincia couldn't quite contain her gasp, which made the woman grin. "I am Catarina Phosythesis Emira. My late father and mother died several years ago, and so I was the appointed head of the Emira Family."

"Oh." Elincia looked away, aghast. "I'm sorry."

The reassuring smile on Catarina's face made Elincia's shoulder relax. "Please do not apologize. There's no need. Come, come. Sit with me."

Elincia and Caspian followed Catarina into a courtyard; the stone steps they walked on were surrounded on either side by flowers, many of which Caspian didn't recognize. They were all colorful, though. He'd never seen such a wide variety of colorful flora before.

Catarina stepped into a small gazebo made of white marble. Sitting down on a stone bench that encircled the inside like a ring, she patted the spot beside her. Elincia sat down. Caspian opted to stand.

"If I am not mistaken, you two are Elincia and Caspian, correct?" Catarina asked, clapping her hands together.

"Um, yes. That's right," Elincia said. She sounded confused. Caspian didn't blame her.

With a prominent smile appearing on her face, Catarina's eyes suddenly gained a vivid luster that hadn't been present before. She took one of Elincia's hands and held it between her generous bosom.

"You don't know how happy I am to meet you two. Because I come from a minor noble house, I was unable to meet with you, but I attended the tournament. In fact, I was one of the people who you, Caspian, rescued when those Murakumos attacked."

"Is that so?" Caspian murmured when she locked eyes with him. "I'm glad that you were able to make it out of there safely."

"As am I," Catarina said. "In either event, I am very pleased to make both of your acquaintances."

"The pleasure is all ours," Elincia said, smiling.

Allowing Elincia to retract her hand, Catarina shifted in her seat as though composing herself after having been discombobulated by her own exuberance. "Now then, what brings you two to this small hamlet? I can't imagine the newest sorceress and knight pair coming all this way for no reason."

"You're right. We do have a reason." Elincia's expression suddenly turned grave. "And it's not a pleasant one."

It took nearly four hours to explain the current situation. Elincia told Catarina about how she and Caspian had been sent there because of the rumors that undead had been spotted in Parumé. She talked about how they had traveled to Exiguus and discovered that the city had been overrun with undead. She even told the young noblewoman what Jessie had told them, about how a lich king had taken up residence either in or somewhere around Parumé.

Because Caspian was a knight, he remained silent throughout the conversation, not daring to speak. Sorceress' knights were not supposed to speak out of turn. They silently dedicated themselves to serving their sorceress, only speaking when directly spoken to. That was how a sorceress's knight was supposed to conduct themselves, according to D'artagnan.

That said, Caspian wasn't really the type to just remain silent and not do anything. On the occasion where Elincia looked at him, as though asking whether or not she had her information correct, Caspian would interject with an anecdote to further extrapolate on certain points that Elincia had made. By the time they were finished, Catarina had been given a concise but lengthy explanation on the current situation.

Her face had grown ghostly pale.

"There's a lich king in the Ruudon Province?" Her voice shook, though not without reason. There had never been a recorded time where a lich king appeared and didn't nearly destroy a country. "H-have you confirmed the existence of this lich king?"

Elincia shook her head. "We haven't seen the lich king for ourselves, but Jessie, the woman from Exiguus, claims to have seen the lich king when her village was attacked."

"This is a serious issue," Catarina proclaimed. "A lich king... I can't believe it."

"I know it's not easy to believe, but it is true," Elincia said with the kind of earnestness that only idealists could match. "Please believe me."

Catarina held up a hand. "I do not doubt your words. I am merely shocked that a lich king would be here. Do you know how long it's been around?"

"Um…" Elincia looked at Caspian.

"There's no way to know for sure whether or not what I am about to tell you is true," Caspian began, taking over for Elincia. "However, I am originally from Parumé, so I believe my words will hold more weight. When I was young, Parumé was destroyed and all of its people were mercilessly slaughtered. People would eventually go on to say that it was due to a bandit raid, but that's not true."

Caspian took a deep breath.

"Parumé was not destroyed in a bandit raid eleven years ago. It was overrun with undead…"

Thus Caspian told the haunting tale of his past underneath a gazebo surrounded by a colorful array of flowers.

Interlude 1

The day after Elincia and Caspian left on their task to deal with the necromancer, Sylvia had begun doing her best to quell the rising sense of discontent among the people. She had publicly announced that Elincia was an elf. Along with the announcement, Sylvia gave everyone the knowledge that Elincia had been forced to abandon her home due to civil strife, and that she was in no danger of betraying them.

It hadn't worked.

The people were still decrying her decision.

Since she had made the official announcement, many of the people in Casadinia had sent her letters. Most of them contained insults, several had questioned her decision to let Elincia become a sorceress, and one had even called her a traitorous rank whore who'd sold herself to the elves. Of the thousands of letters she received, only a handful spoke in support of her decision.

I do not understand...

For the whole of her life, Sylvia had dedicated herself toward the betterment of humanity. Every decision she had made, from rallying humanity under one banner, fighting against the elves, defeating the nobility and dismantling Terraria's military, to making education compulsory for both peasants and nobles, all of it had been done to give humans a better world to live in.

So why? Why did these people call her a traitor? Why could they not see what she was trying to accomplish?

Why would they say I betrayed them to join the elves?

It made no sense. True, Sylvia wanted to bridge the gap between humans and elves. She believed their two races could learn a lot from each other.

Elves were a race who had an unnatural affinity for nature. Their long lives granted them wisdom that humans could never acquire, their magic gave them abilities that were far more varied than those of a sorceress', and they knew more about this world than many other species.

Humans were capable of adapting to almost any circumstance, were capable of harnessing great power, and contained some of the most inventive people she knew. It was thanks to human ingenuity that Casadinia had become such a grand city. It was thanks to human adaptability that they had weathered so many storms. In return for having shorter lives, humans had gained a desire to progress their civilization that elves lacked.

Each species had their strong points and weak points. If they combined forces, if they learned to live alongside one another, she was positive they could reach even greater heights.

Sylvia wanted what was best for humanity, what was best for this world, which was also why she did her best to dissociate herself from her emotions. If she allowed herself to feel, then she was liable to do what was best for herself and not what was best for others. This was how she had accomplished so much, from forming the Sorceress Council to creating the Peacekeepers, a powerful law enforcement group of elite warriors who didn't respond to the council's will. She would not have been able to accomplishing everything she had if she let her emotions rule her.

For over one thousand years, she had served humanity.

So why?

Why was she being called a traitor now?

"You're nothing but a deluded old hag. You clearly don't understand humans half as well as you think you do. I pity you, Sylvia."

The words of Erica during one of their meetings nearly made her scowl.

Erica had always told her that she was out of touch with humanity, that she didn't understand humans, and that she probably never would. That egotistical woman took great pleasure in informing her about her deficiencies as a human every chance she got. She hadn't done so in a while, but that was merely because she and Erica had not met in several months.

Her office was quiet as she sat behind her desk, dictating several notes onto a parchment filled with half-formed ideas. She was trying to think up a method of quelling the rising discontent. Nothing she had attempted worked so far, but she believed that was merely because the news was still fresh in people's minds. Perhaps if she left this matter alone for a few more weeks, things would settle down on their own—but no. If she did that, it could cause more problems.

Sylvia sighed.

She was not alone in her office. D'artagnan stood behind her, a silent sentinel.

A large stack of letters sat on her desk. They were the many complaints about Elincia, which she had no intention of looking at anymore, since all of them said the same thing.

Her magicom buzzed, static crackled from the speaker, and then a voice emerged. *"Lady Sylvia, Count De'Falco is here and says he would like to speak with you."*

She frowned at the magicom. Her mind was awhirl with thoughts.

What does that man want now?

She pressed the talk button and said, "send him in."

"Yes, ma'am."

"D'artagnan," Sylvia said. The creaking of leather armor behind her let her know that D'Artagnan was listening. "Watch Count De'Falco closely during this meeting. After what happened with Matthew Davidson, I suspect he might be involved in the illegal manufacturing of Murakumos."

Count De'Falco had managed to avoid getting persecuted by claiming plausible deniability. Unfortunately, he had evidence to support that he had no idea what was going on underneath the building of his own headquarters. At the same time, she couldn't believe that a man like him didn't know what had happened. It was too suspicious.

"I will do as you say, My Lady."

The door opened after their conversation had finished, and Count Callisto De'Falco Genitore entered the room. His shoulder-length blond hair swayed as he walked. That evening, he wore a dark purple doublet and black pants with leather boots. A shoulder cape the same color as his pants swished when he performed a flourishing bow.

"Lady Sylvia." Count De'Falco looked up, blue eyes hidden behind several strands of hair. "It's very good to see you again. I apologize for not coming sooner, but I have had my hands full trying to weed out the corruption in my company."

"So I have heard," Sylvia responded coolly. "Is there a particular reason for your visit today?"

"Indeed there is." Straightening, Count De'Falco pierced Sylvia with a somber stare. "I wanted to offer my condolences on what happened with your newest sorceress. I feel responsible for the whole incident. After all, it was my company that Lady Elincia was investigating when her secret was uncovered. I wish to make up for what happened by lending you my aid."

At the count's offer of help, Sylvia couldn't help but feel suspicious, especially because while she didn't hate nobles, she also understood that nobles never did anything if it didn't benefit themselves. That was why she had dismantled their government. On the other hand, she couldn't afford to spurn his offer for aid. Count De'Falco was one of the highest-ranking nobles in Arcadia. One did not reject such an offer when it was given.

"What sort of help did you have in mind?" asked Sylvia.

"People tend to change opinions quickly based on their perceptions of others," Count De'Falco said. "Right now, many people dislike Elincia because she is an elf, but that could change if she performed a great service for the people."

"A great service, you say?" Sylvia frowned.

The count nodded. "Indeed, a great service. For example: if she were to weed out corruption among the nobles, it would go a long way toward fixing her reputation, especially if the noble in question was involved in slave trading."

Sylvia did not reveal her emotions, but she felt wary of this man's suggestion, though she couldn't deny the truth of his words. Opinions could be changed when someone performed a great deed, such as when Caspian protected so many people from the Murakumos during tournament. The question was what could Elincia do, what great deed could she perform, to regain the trust of the people?

Her frown deepened. "You specifically mentioned slave trading. Are you telling me that there is a noble who is involved in the slave trade?"

"I know of several." With another flourish, Count De'Falco produced a scroll from a pouch on his hip. He presented the scroll to Sylvia, who laid it on the desk and unfurled it. "I've been investigating this matter for several years now. Several of my staff members are former slaves, so I felt it was my duty to help. This is a list of all the names I've uncovered."

Several names were written in neat cursive. Marquis Hunington. Marquis Nivan. Duke Thistlethane. Viscount Madrid. Baron Gerosso. There were around twenty-five names in total.

Sylvia did not recognize any of them, but that no longer

surprised her. So many nobles had come and gone that she'd stopped remembering the names of every single one.

"This is a rather extensive list."

"It should be. I've spent around four years making it."

"We will have to check the authenticity of this list." Sylvia held the list out to D'artagnan. The man gingerly took it off her hands and studied the list. His leather armor creaked some more.

"I would expect no less." Count De'Falco bowed before them. "I hope this information comes in handy. Should you ever have need of me, please let me know. I am more than willing to lend you a hand."

"I see." Sylvia grew silent for a moment. "I appreciate the offer. If I am ever in need of your services, I will be sure to get in contact with you."

Count De'Falco smiled. "That is all I ask. Now, if you'll excuse me, I actually have to leave Casadinia for a while. I have some business to attend to at the Avrondale Mines. Please contact my aid should you require my services."

The count left soon after, and as the door closed behind him, Sylvia frowned, unsure of what to make of that parting statement. She put it out of her mind, however. The count's itinerary wasn't something that she needed to be concerned about.

"Did you notice anything off about him?" she asked D'artagnan.

"Only that he is traveling to the Avrondale Mines," D'artagnan said as he continued to stare at the names on the parchment. "That's located in Lady Erica's territory, and it's quite far from Casadinia. I cannot fathom what purpose he might have for going there himself when he could just as easily send a representative."

"They did hit a recent spirit crystal vein," Sylvia hypothesized. "He might be going there to negotiate exclusive rights, and since the issue with Davidson, he might have trouble trusting his own people."

"Perhaps."

"Anything else?"

D'artagnan shook his head. "No. I couldn't detect a lie in any of his words."

"Neither could I."

But that just made Sylvia more concerned. As a sorceress with over one thousand years of experience, she could spot a lie regardless how well someone tried to hide it, and thus far, every noble she had ever met lied through their teeth. That neither she nor D'artagnan could detect a lie from Count De'Falco was disconcerting.

"What do you make of the names on that scroll?" she asked.

"I recognize many of them." D'artagnan set the scroll on the desk and crossed his arms. "Several of them are hardliner noble families who had opposed the dissolution of the House of Lords. They capitulated after your victory during the Succession War. However, I doubt these families would so easily reform. It would not surprise me if many of them were sanctioning or participating in illegal acts like slavery."

With a thoughtful hum, Sylvia debated on what to do about this. After a moment, she said, "send that list to the Peacekeepers and request that they investigate these individuals. If it turns out that these nobles are indeed committing crimes, then we can send Elincia to deal with them when she and Caspian return."

She didn't trust Count De'Falco, but if nothing else, she agreed that the best way to change people's opinions was to show Elincia in the best light possible. Having her strike down criminals responsible for kidnapping and slave trading would go a long way toward doing just that.

Sylvia withheld a sigh and grabbed the next scroll that she needed to look over. She put it on the desk and unfurled it, letting the contents be seen, and then—

There was a knock on the door.

"Come in," Sylvia called.

"Excuse me," Lacy said as she entered the room. She walked forward, hands clasped in front of her. It wasn't until she stood in front of the desk that Sylvia noticed the letter in her hands. "I apologize for the intrusion, My Lady, but this letter came in just a little while ago. It's from Elincia, so I thought it might be important."

"I see. Thank you."

Sylvia took the letter from Lacy. The envelope was yellow, the parchment aged, and when she opened the envelope and took out the letter, she noticed that the paper quality they used was cheap and old. Wrinkles covered the paper, and there were several stains as though ink had been spilled on it. Fortunately, it was still legible.

Lady Sylvia,

Parumé and its surrounding villages have become overrun with undead. A lich king has made its base somewhere near the village. We are requesting another sorceress to aid us in expelling the threat.

Signed,

Elincia

The letter was short, to the point, and announced that there were far more problems than Sylvia had realized.

A lich king. They were perhaps one of the most dangerous creatures alive. Sylvia had once fought against a lich king centuries ago and the battle had nearly killed her. She had only been able to survive thanks to her knight at the time, who had sacrificed his life so she could chant a seventy-five-verse aria, her longest one ever.

"D'artagnan," Sylvia said quietly, "which sorceress lives closest to Parumé?"

After a moment of silence, D'artagnan said, "the closest sorceress to Parumé is Maddison Vermone."

"She's a relatively new sorceress," Sylvia murmured, resisting the urge to bite her lip. Maddison wouldn't be much help on her own, since her knight was not selected from the Sorceress' Knight Tournament, but from the Peacekeepers who had graduated from the academy. There was also the fact that they hadn't heard from her in over five years. "Who else is near Parumé?"

"If you are looking for a powerful sorceress who can help deal with a threat of this caliber, the only one that I can think of is Erica Demonica de Angelo," D'artagnan said.

Sylvia didn't want to contact Erica for anything. She certainly didn't want to ask that woman for help. Not only was the idea of asking Erica to go and support Elincia humiliating, but the other sorceress was bound to gloat about how "the great Sylvia" had begged her to aid Elincia. The idea was almost retching.

"Prepare the communication mirror," Sylvia said at last, standing up as her expression settled into one of polite indifference. "We're going to contact Erica and ask her to meet up with and aid Elincia in defeating the lich king."

"Yes, My Lady."

As she and D'artagnan left the office and walked down the hall, traveling toward the communications room, Sylvia prepared to shunt aside her personal distaste of the woman she was about to speak with.

She had to remain objective.

A lich king was too great a threat to allow her personal feelings to get in the way.

This was just another way in which Sylvia purged her emotions for the greater good.

Chapter 7

Caspian and Elincia spoke with Catarina well into the evening. By the time they had finished, the sky had turned dark and the stars had come out. Chilly midnight air made goosebumps break out on their flesh.

Catarina had listened to their story with a serious frown marring her face the entire time, not asking a single question until after they had finished. When Elincia stopped talking, the young noble leaned back, took a deep breath, and sighed.

"That is a very grim story you've just told me," she said at last. "If it were anyone else, I probably wouldn't have believed them, or simply believed that person was maybe hallucinating… but I can tell that neither of you are lying, which means our situation will become dire soon if we don't do anything."

"I sense some hesitation in your words," Caspian said, no longer acting as a proper knight should as he took part in this conversation.

A smile on her face, Catarina shrugged. "At the moment, there is not much we can do. Even if I was inclined to evacuate this entire city, we can't do that at the present time, especially since it is so late." She paused and stared at her cup of now cold tea. "I would like to speak with you both more tomorrow regarding this subject. For now, I believe we should get some rest. You two have been through a lot, and I think a good night's sleep will help."

While Caspian didn't know if that was the best idea, as he felt haste was their greatest ally right then, he also knew that he didn't have any right to complain, especially when Elincia agreed with her.

"We can pick this up tomorrow," Elincia agreed.

"Then please let me show you to your rooms."

Catarina stood up and gestured for them to follow her. Caspian was still a little surprised that a noble would be tending to her guests in such a manner. Where were all her servants? He didn't say anything as he and Elincia followed the woman back inside of the mansion, but he couldn't deny that he was curious.

"By the way," Catarina began as they wandered up the sweeping staircase in the foyer. "Do you two want a room together, or do you sleep separately?"

The question wasn't startling, though it was embarrassing. There were many occasions where sorceresses and knights fell in love, or at least became lovers, such as the case with Erica and Derek, but there were also many sorceresses and knights who saw their relationship as one that was strictly business. The type of relationship shared was always determined by the sorceress and the knight.

Caspian wished he could speak telepathically to Elincia, but they weren't touching just then, and he didn't know if holding her hand would give Catarina the wrong impression… or would that be the right impression? This whole matter was one that he was embarrassed by.

"Um… if you don't mind, I would prefer if we only had o-one bedroom," Elincia said, only stuttering a bit. She couldn't quite contain her blush, however, and a light hue of red spread across her cheeks and the bridge of her nose.

Catarina grinned. "Sure thing! Just follow me."

They turned down a long hallway with several doors. Elincia walked beside Catarina. Caspian hung back and observed their surroundings, noting the distinct absence of expensive artwork. Once again, the only decorations were the vases filled with flowers.

"Um, do you mind if I ask where all of your servants are?" asked Elincia.

"Oh, I don't have any," Catarina responded with a brilliant smile that reminded Caspian of sunflowers. "My last servant died of old age a few months ago. Afterward, I decided to periodically hire people from the town when I needed help instead of relying on a servant. I always choose a different person each time. It's nice because it allows me to meet the people I govern, and they get to meet me."

"I see," Elincia said for lack of having anything better to say.

Caspian actually thought it was a good idea. Allowing different people to work for her for one day meant she not only met many different people, but her subjects could get to know her more intimately, which meant that she was more than just a faceless lord ruling them from on high.

It wasn't often that he felt respect for nobles, but in this case, Caspian believed that Catarina was deserving of respect.

"And here we are." Catarina opened a door to their left and gestured for them to enter. "This will be your room for the night. I hope it's to your liking."

"Thank you," Caspian said.

"We appreciate you allowing us to stay the night," Elincia added.

Catarina, still smiling, replied, "Not at all! It's nice to have some company for a change. Please sleep well."

Comfortable was the first word that came to mind as Caspian stepped into the room with Elincia. It wasn't large like his room at Sylvia's mansion, but it wasn't small either. It looked around the same size as the one he had at the academy, except since there was only one bed, it appeared a bit bigger. There were only a few furnishings outside of the bed. Oddly enough, the room had its own fireplace.

"Feel free to stay here for now," Catarina said. "If you'd like, I can come get you in about an hour and we can have dinner, but I need to prepare it first."

It was a bit late for dinner, but at the mention of it, both his and Elincia's stomachs rumbled. Elincia held a hand to her stomach and blushed. Caspian didn't, but that was mostly because of Catarina's words, or what he inferred from her words.

"You cook your own meals?" Caspian couldn't contain his surprise, even though, logically speaking, it was obvious that she cooked her own meals. She didn't have any servants, after all.

"Yes," Catarina said. "I have been cooking since I was young. I've always loved it. In either event, I'll get you when it's time for dinner."

"Thank you," Elincia said as she mastered her blush.

Catarina gave them one last smile, and then left the room, shutting the door with a soft *click*.

Now alone in the room, Caspian wondered what he should do. He wanted to do something, but…

Confidence, Caspian. You two have already taken a good leap in your relationship. You need to have confidence.

"Well," Elincia began as she placed her hands on her hips and tried to feign nonchalance, "I guess there's not much that we can do right—kya! C-Caspian?!"

Elincia's surprised squeal resounded around the room as Caspian hugged her from behind. With her warm, soft body in his arms, Caspian allowed his feelings to intertwine with hers. Their bond was flaring to life, sending emotions into him that belonged to Elincia and vice versa. He could tell what she was thinking. She was not displeased by his actions, so he felt no need to let go.

He placed his chin on her head. "Just let me stay like this for a while."

"O-okay," Elincia mumbled. Despite her embarrassment, which

rang clear through the bond, she let him hold her, and she even placed her hands over his arms as though to keep them there.

Alone in that room, Caspian and Elincia enjoyed this short moment of peace.

***

When Catarina had said that she could cook, Caspian assumed she would only know how to make simple meals. He was proven wrong. That night, she had made cheese ravioli with fresh tomato and artichoke sauce. It had been delicious, a flavorful dish that neither he nor Elincia could stop eating until their stomachs were fit to bursting. They had complimented Catarina on her cooking, to which she had responded with a wonderful smile and a gracious thank you.

Their bellies full, Caspian and Elincia had gone off to bed again. It was awkward at first, sleeping in the same bed, which they were still not used to. Neither of them knew what to do.

"Are you still awake, Caspian?"

"I am. What's wrong? Can't sleep?"

The bed shifted when Elincia moved as though trying to get more comfortable. Despite not facing her, he was distinctly aware of her presence at his back.

"I'm too nervous."

"I know how you feel."

He and Elincia were lying on their sides, facing away from each other. He could feel Elincia's warmth on his back, which was barely touching hers. They could have probably used telepathy to talk, but neither of them seemed capable of working up the courage, perhaps because they could feel each other's mutual embarrassment and uncertainty flowing into them through the bond. It was hard to tell who was feeling what emotion with their minds congealing together like this.

"I'm beginning to wonder if this might have been a mistake," Elincia admitted. "I wanted to share a bed with you because I thought it would make us closer, but now all I can think about is how embarrassed I am."

115

Caspian understood how she felt perfectly. It was true that they had been sleeping together the other night, but both of them had been too exhausted to care, and they had also had the excuse of sleeping together to share body heat. There was no such readily available excuse now.

What should I do?

Something needed to be done, if not because Caspian didn't want their relationship to remain like this, then because he was honestly sick of being so embarrassed all the time. He wanted to be able to hold her in his arms. He didn't want to be ashamed of wanting to be physically close to her. They were each other's everything, weren't they? Shouldn't they be allowed to hug and cuddle and kiss all they wanted? Why was this so hard?

"Look here, Boy! Elincia's not going to push your relationship to new heights. She's not going to help it advance. It's not in a woman's nature. If you want to become closer and take that next step, then you have to be the one who does it! Women like a man who knows how to take charge!"

The words of Sebastian came to him, filtering through his mind as though they were coming from a vast distance. Perhaps the old man had a point. Maybe he needed to take the lead. Would Elincia like it if he did? He didn't know, but…

Oh, screw it.

Acting quickly, Caspian turned around, wrapped an arm around Elincia's waist, and pulled her until her back was pressing against his chest.

Elincia squeaked. "C-Caspian?! What are you—"

"I just… want to be closer to you," Caspian muttered through the embarrassing red haze of his mind.

"Oh…" Elincia paused. "W-well… that's okay, I guess. I want to be closer to you, too."

"Is this uncomfortable?"

"N-no. It's nice." While it took some time, Elincia eventually relaxed against him, and she scooted backwards as though to close the remaining distance between them. Now with her back firmly pressed against his chest, the two of them could feel even more of each other, both physically and emotionally. "Very nice. I really like this. It feels like…"

"Like my arms were made to hold you?"

"… Yes."

"I'm glad."

No more words were spoken, and a steady silence reigned in the room. Caspian listened to the small noises around them—the wind as it rattled against the window, the stirring of the curtains, and Elincia's soft breathing. It looked like she had already fallen asleep. He closed his eyes and slowly let sleep take him.

There was no telling how long he slept. It felt like only a few seconds had passed since he closed his eyes when the door to their room burst open. Hurried footsteps thudded against the floor. There was more than one set. Caspian, startled awake by the noise, counted three footsteps in total.

Assassins?

Caspian released Elincia and tried to leap to his feet, but, sadly, his feet became tangled in the bed sheets. Instead of looking cool as he prepared for combat, he fell face first onto the floor. It hurt. His face stung. He was sure that his nose was also red from having been rubbed against the carpet. His face was burning with shame, invisible to everyone as he laid there on the floor.

Scrambling to his feet, knowing that he couldn't afford to let his humiliation stop him, Caspian reached for his sword, which sat in its sheath against the nightstand. He stopped when he saw who was standing there.

It was Catarina. Her cheeks were flushed from having run all the way here, and her chest heaved as she took several lungfuls of air. She looked like she was on the verge of panicking.

"We have a problem!" she said to them, and the urgency in her tone caused the hairs on his neck to stand on end. Her shout caused

Elincia to jerk upright and look around. The pretty blonde's eyes landed on Catarina.

"What's wrong?" Caspian asked, strapping on his sheath as Elincia stumbled out of bed.

"Flos is under attack," Catarina said in a hurry. "It happened so fast! We're being attacked by undead!"

If Caspian hadn't been awake already, then he certainly was now. Even though there had been a high possibility of an undead attack, he was shocked by how quickly it had happened, and there was also the timing to consider. Was this a random attack? Had the lich king decided to expand its territory? Or had the lich king tracked him and Elincia after they escaped from Exiguus?

Caspian shook the thoughts off. *It doesn't matter why they're here now. We need to hurry.*

"If undead are attacking, then the first thing we need to do is halt their advance," Caspian said, adjusting his sheath for easy access. "Where are they attacking from?"

"From the east entrance," Catarina said.

"Caspian and I will go there and push them back," Elincia said, now fully awake. "Catarina, why don't you—"

"I'm going with you," Catarina interrupted. "These are my people. It's my duty to protect them, so I'm not going to run and hide while you two go off and fight on your own." As if to emphasize her point, Catarina pulled up her pink dress, revealing the two pistols strapped to her thighs. "I might not be able to fight like either of you, but I'm a decent shot."

Guns were a relatively new invention. They were not magical— not all of them. Most of them relied on a flintlock system; the flintlock mechanism was drawn back and struck the gunpowder inside of the pistol, which produced a spark, and the spark caused the gunpowder to ignite and shoot a led projectile. Of course, there were magical guns that used magical technology, but only the highest-ranking Peacekeepers and high-class nobles owned those.

The two that Catarina had under her dress were elegant, but they were still only standard flintlock pistols. That meant she had a limited amount of ammo.

"That's—" Elincia started to say.

"That's fine," Caspian said before Elincia could tell Catarina that she couldn't come with them. Elincia looked in his direction, wearing a frown that all but asked why he was disputing her. He shook his head. "We don't have time to argue, and she can be a big help to us by providing long range support." He turned back to Catarina—more specifically, the two behind her. "You two! I'm guessing you're the ones who informed Catarina of this? Go back out and escort however many people you can to this mansion."

"Why here?" asked Catarina.

"Because the lich king has thousands of undead at his beck and call. If we're being attacked on one side, it's only a matter of time before we'll be attacked on all sides. That being the case, if your people are spread out across Flos, it will be harder to protect them."

His grim proclamation was met with silence. The two men shook. Catarina's face was pale, but she admirably recovered, lips becoming a thin line as her eyes glinted with determination.

"I understand." She turned to the two men. "Escort our people to this mansion. We'll protect them from here."

There was little time left. Undead were practically on their doorstep, so everyone quickly agreed to his plan. This time, Caspian was the one who led Catarina and Elincia outside. Screams were already piercing the night sky in the distance. Two kilometers out, near the eastern entrance where Caspian and Elincia had first arrived, he could make out the figures of Flos's citizens as they ran every which way in a panic, and also…

With his elvish vision, Caspian could easily see the undead as they tore into human flesh.

Chapter 8

The closer Caspian, Catarina, and Elincia got to the eastern side of Flos, the harder it became for them to move. Hundreds of people pushed and shoved against them, all in an effort to escape from the undead. They were traveling against the flow as it were.

Caspian grunted as people flew into him. He stumbled as bodies both big and small bashed against him like waves crashing against the shore. Everyone was screaming, a threnody of terrified voices that stabbed his ears like a knife and resounded in his soul. Elincia had it even worse with her smaller body and more sensitive hearing.

"It's too difficult to move like this!" Elincia shouted to be overheard.

"I won't be able to shoot my guns with so many people around!" Catarina seemingly agreed as she screamed over the roar of frightened civilians.

Caspian ground his teeth together as he quickly thought about how he could get past these people. An idea quickly sprang to mind, though he didn't like it.

It's not like I have a choice, though.

"I'm going on ahead," Caspian told them. He didn't give them a chance to reply. The longer they were stuck like this, the more people would be killed. "Springen!"

Leaping off the ground thanks to the power of his spell, Caspian easily soared over the heads of the panicked humans. He landed on a nearby building covered in flowers. Springing off of it with another magically aided leap, he traveled all the way to where the undead were attacking.

It was a massacre. Those who were unlucky enough to be in the back of the panicking crowd were getting torn apart. Undead swarmed over the humans who had fallen. Limbs were torn off bodies in a crimson spray that splattered the ground. The screams here were not just those of terror, but of pain. Of agony. It was a sound that made it feel like icy stakes were being driven into his heart.

"Springen!"

Caspian launched himself at a group of undead surrounding a human who had yet to be killed. His sword swing took off a head. His second swing, aided by magic, split another undead in half. Spinning around on the balls of his feet, he didn't give the last undead a chance to even notice him before he rammed his blade through the monster's jaw, straight into its brain, killing it.

"You there!" Caspian shouted as he yanked his sword from the undead, ignoring the lump of flesh as it hit the ground with a meaty thump. "Get moving!"

The man that he had rescued didn't need any more prompting than that. Screaming as though his life had just flashed before his eyes, he scrambled to his feet and ran like hellhounds were nipping at his heels.

Caspian didn't wait around and watch; there were still hundreds of undead to kill and plenty of people who needed to be rescued. Launching himself forward with a war cry, Caspian lost himself in the heat of battle.

The night was soon painted in red.

*****

"Thor! Please help me!"

Lightning rained down from the heavens, slamming into nearly a dozen undead, cooking them from the inside out. The scent of sizzling flesh filled the air. Elincia wrinkled her nose, resisted the urge to vomit, and, with a grim expression marring her face, she continued attacking her foes with the aid of Thor.

Accompanying her magical attacks was Catarina's pistols. *Bang! Bang bang bang!* When Catarina had said that she was a good shot, Elincia had not believed she would be this amazing. Every bullet fired struck an undead in the skull, penetrating their head and killing them instantly. The woman attacked from a distance, firing at an almost constant rate. She only stopped when she needed to reload.

The crowd had thinned out around them, leaving only a few terrified civilians in the area—the ones who she and Catarina were protecting. Up ahead, his sword swinging as he danced through his opponents, Caspian had committed himself fully to battle. His blade sung. Heads rolled. Bodies were split. Her knight was a whirlwind of vicious combat.

However, not even Caspian could deal with a horde this massive on his own. He needed help.

"Freya, please lend me something to help Caspian with."

Light coalesced into her hand. Something heavy made her arm sag. A spear had appeared in her hand, elegant and gleaming a bright silver. Hundreds of runes were inscribed onto the spear's surface, creating a myriad of patterns until the shaft ended and the blade began. As she held the spear in her hand, Elincia felt something come up behind her, a familiar presence.

Freya, spirit of battle and fertility, was lending Elincia her strength.

Her arm was pulled back, controlled by a will that was not her own. Elincia felt the other hand over hers, directing her, guiding her. With Freya helping her, Elincia threw the spear. It shot from her hand

far more quickly than she anticipated. Light burst from the tip, arcs of archaic energy that struck the undead that the spear shot past. Heads exploded. Bodies had holes blown through them. Still the spear continued on, bursting through multiple undead until, having run out of mana, the spear dispersed into particles.

The presence of Freya behind her disappeared, her task done.

Elincia was given a short moment of reprieve. There were no undead near her. That last attack had cleared them all away, and so she could observe the battlefield as she caught her breath.

It was a horrible sight.

Like something out of a nightmare, dead bodies lay strewn about, some of which weren't entirely whole, having been torn apart by the undead. Crimson ran through the streets. The scent of iron tickled her nose, making her want to gag. The numerous corpses created a horrific scene that made Elincia turn green. Even during the tournament, when the Murakumos had invaded the colosseum, things hadn't been this bad.

Knowing that she couldn't stand idly by, Elincia threw herself back into the battle. Blood and violence became her companions once again.

***

Time lost its meaning as Caspian tore through the undead like he was the scythe and they the wheat. All he knew was blood. The scent of it stung his nose, the sight of it burned his eyes, and the feel of it splattering against his clothing made him want to hurl. Even so, he kept on fighting. His body moved of its own accord, swinging, hacking, slashing, all the while moving inexorably closer to Elincia and Catarina.

Behead an undead. Take a step back. Move forward. Sidestep. Thrust.

It was almost mindless, the way he killed the undead surrounding him. None of them had any intelligence. They were just bodies being controlled from a distance. There was no sense of tactics to their attacks. They came at him and were cut down with an ease that was almost laughable.

Except Caspian could find nothing funny about this situation.

"Halkaista!"

Caspian swung his sword as he spun in a full circle. With his blade's sharpness enhanced to the point where not even bricks could give him trouble, Caspian cut straight through all of the undead around him like a letter opener tearing through an envelope. Heads were severed and flew off, striking the ground and rolling away. Bodies dropped as blood spurted from severed limbs. An arm flew off. An undead woman was disslegged. Another person was bisected from their hips to their shoulders.

He moved on without glancing back.

There were still undead to kill.

A scream from down an alley forced Caspian to change course, away from Elincia, who was busy blasting undead apart with lightning and light-based attacks. Portals to another dimension, a different plane of existence, opened all around his sorceress as Thor and Baldr aided her with long-range fire.

He rushed through the alley until he reached a dead end. A little girl had her back against the wall. Four undead were stalking toward her.

"Springen!"

His leap took him all the way to the girl. He landed in front of her, and, spinning like a ballerina, he swung his blade through the first undead's neck. The others turned their attention to him as the one he killed dropped to the ground. A moment passed in which the three merely stared at him, as if they couldn't comprehend what another person was doing in front of them. Then the moment passed.

They lunged. He dodged.

Caspian took three steps back to avoid being touched. Then he placed all of his weight onto his left foot, building up kinetic energy, which he used to launch himself forward.

"Halkaista!"

Two steps took him into the undead's guard. He swung. Then he was moving past the undead, which split into two separate pieces.

Spinning around, he attacked an undead that was on his left, felt a moment of resistance, and then cut through the creature's body, furrowing a large trench from shoulder to groin. He beheaded it after that.

The last undead wasn't even given time to attack; Caspian split its head open like cutting through an overripe fruit. It fell to the ground, coagulated blood oozing from its skull.

He took a moment to regain himself. A red haze had been cast over his eyes, slowly dissipating as he became more aware of his surroundings. Finally, after calming his racing heart, he turned to the girl.

"Are you okay, little one?" Caspian asked.

The girl didn't respond with words. She just cried.

I don't have time to deal with this.

Caspian wanted to reassure her, but he needed to get back to Elincia. Who knew what was happening without him. She only had a limited amount of mana.

"Sorry," he apologized as he picked the girl up and slung her over his shoulder like she was a sack of flour. "But I'm in a bit of a hurry. I'll get you somewhere safe, so please just be patient until then."

Oddly enough, the girl stopped crying after he finished speaking. She did sniffle a few times, but that was it. With a now mostly silent child on one shoulder, Caspian ran back to where he had left Elincia and Catarina.

***

Elincia was gasping, sucking in deep, ragged breaths by the time all of the undead in their vicinity were killed. Her chest ached. Sweat trailed down her skin and soaked into her clothes, the fabric of which clung to her body, making for an unpleasant sensation. She knew she shouldn't have worn a dress.

The corpses of those she had slain laid all around her. A sea of bodies and blood. The walls of nearby buildings were painted red. By this point, Elincia had become so inured to all the death that she barely paid it any attention.

The realization that she was now used to this made her squeamish.

"I think that's the last group over here," Catarina said as she wiped the sweat from her brow. "We should head to the next street over. There are still plenty of undead attacking my people."

Her guns were smoking. Catarina had proven herself an able shooter, and in fact, it was thanks to her amazing aim that Elincia was still alive. Several times she might have died were it not for the woman's ability to shoot an undead in the head at a twenty-meter range.

"Right." Elincia nodded in agreement, though she was worried. Her mana reserves had taken a major hit. She only had enough for a few more partial summons, and she wouldn't be able to perform a full summon, not even if she dispelled the illusion around her ears.

"Elincia! Catarina!" Caspian called out as he ran out from between two buildings. He was carrying a small child over his shoulders, a little girl with pigtails who couldn't have been more than seven or eight, ten at the most.

"So that's what you were doing when you ran off," Catarina said. She put her fists on her hips. "I hadn't realized there was a child in that alley. Good save."

"I heard her scream," he said, setting the young girl back on the ground. She wobbled a bit, but Caspian held her steady by placing a hand on her back as he knelt down. "Are you okay?"

The girl sniffled, nodded, and then asked, "where's my mommy?"

"I don't know," Caspian answered, "but we'll do everything we can to find her."

"I can take her to where the others are being evacuated into my mansion." Catarina held her hand out to the little girl. There was a moment's hesitation before the child took the offered hand. Catarina cast the two a grave expression as she said, "Athrun and Kira should still be near the end of this road. I'll hand her off to them, and then meet up with you two afterward."

"That sounds good," Caspian agreed.

"Be careful," Elincia added.

"Will do. Come on, little one."

With the little girl in tow, Catarina trotted off toward the end of this road. In the silence that followed, Caspian turned to Elincia.

"How are you feeling?" he asked.

"I'm almost out of mana." Elincia closed her eyes, shoulders drooping as she fought against her exhaustion. She took a deep breath. Then, dredging up what energy she could muster, Elincia straightened her spine. "However, I can't leave things as they are. Even if I can only use a few more partial summons, that'll mean a few more people who would've died will get to live."

"Well said." Caspian reached out and took her hand. "I'll be with you every step of the way. Leave the heavy fighting to me. You can conserve your mana for when we really need it."

"Thank you."

"Anytime."

With the night still young, the screams and howls of horrified people still filling the air, Caspian and Elincia went off to find more people who needed saving.

130

Chapter 9

When Caspian had said that he would do the heavy fighting, he hadn't known at the time what that would entail.

Duck. Swing. Behead an undead. Blood sprayed the ground and Caspian's clothing.

Now fighting against a seemingly endless horde of undead, he was coming to the realization that he himself might be the one getting overwhelmed.

Spin. Cut. Slice. Stab. An undead was coming up behind him. Move left. Swing. An arm flew off.

There was no end to the undead that attacked him. They came in from all directions now, and Caspian realized that his earlier prediction, where he had stated that Flos would likely be surrounded, might very well be true. If that was the case, all they could do was retreat into Catarina's mansion and hope the undead were incapable of breaching the walls.

But before that, they would need to rescue as many people as they could.

Undead were created through necromancy. The necromancer would cast a spell on a once living body, bringing it back to life by tethering mana to its brain. Like this, undead could be controlled as though they were puppets.

There was another method of creating undead, and that was for the undead themselves to inject their blood into a human. This could be done through biting or any number of other methods. Outside of it simply being the right thing to do, it was important to save as many people as possible so as to prevent more undead from being created.

Caspian strained his muscles as he swung his blade once more. A crimson spray flew from the throat of an undead, the skin and muscles peeling back as it fell to the ground. Gritting his teeth at the smell, Caspian ignored the now defeated creature and, with a shout of effort, he swung his sword again as more undead came for him—and Elincia, who stood behind him.

He stepped back, and then moved left, dodging an aimless undead that had lunged at him. As he spun around, Caspian swung his sword. It came down from above, sliced through the muscle, organs, and bones in the undead's neck. The creature's head fell off. Its body struck the ground. Sadly, he didn't have time to celebrate his victory.

More undead closed in.

"There are so many!" Elincia shouted as Caspian continued to fight.

"I know!" he shouted back.

"Are you sure I shouldn't call for help?!"

"Not yet! We have no idea how large this horde is! If you call for help now, you might run out of mana when we really need it!"

He understood how Elincia felt, but for the moment, she needed to conserve her strength. She was their trump card.

They were not alone. There were numerous civilians traveling behind them, some carrying pitchforks and hoes, but most were unarmed. Scared mothers held their equally frightened children. Men young and old did what they could to help Caspian fend off the horde. He was grateful for the help, but that said, even with their strength in numbers, they provided little aid.

Elincia and Caspian did everything they could to protect the people who were traveling with them. They directed the civilians up the hill upon which Catarina's mansion sat, fighting against the undead that attacked them. Since Elincia was conserving her mana, he was doing most of the fighting.

Caspian's blade was barely a glimmer of light as he carved through the numerous foes before him, dancing and slashing in an endless waltz of death. He wove his blade in intricate patterns. The sword cleaved through flesh, muscle, and bone, enhanced by his spell, Halkaista, one of his only three spells.

He was tiring. It was just a small ache right now, a simple weariness in his arms, but Caspian knew his own body well enough to understand his limits. He wouldn't be able to keep up this pace for much longer. This was especially true if he used more magic.

Bangbangbangbang!

A quick succession of gunfire like crackling thunder echoed through the area. Four undead went down, blood spurting from small holes on their heads. Glancing to his left, Caspian was just in time to spot Catarina rushing down from the hill, her skirt fluttering about her feet as she fired her pistols in rapid succession.

Bangbangbangbangbangbang!

Six more undead were felled in so little time Caspian would have missed it if he blinked.

"Elincia! Caspian! Hurry up and get everyone inside, and then get inside yourselves!" Catarina shouted.

Even if they wanted to deny her (there were probably still people in the city who needed to be rescued, after all), neither of them were foolish enough to believe they could do anything more. Caspian was running on fumes. Elincia might have enough mana left over for a few partial summons, but she would exhaust herself soon after and become defenseless.

"I'll cover everyone!" Caspian shouted as he sidestepped to the left, swung his blade, and cleaved off the arm of an undead that moved past him. He followed through on his attack by cutting off its head.

Before they could run up the hill to the mansion, the hair on Caspian's neck prickled and his body felt a jolt, instincts warning him that something was coming.

He spun around just as something slammed into the ground several meters away. The ground broke apart. A shockwave rushed out from the center of impact, slamming into him and the others. Screams echoed all around him.

Stumbling backward, Caspian covered his face with his arms, gritting his teeth as several chunks of cobblestone pelted his body.

Lowering his arms, Caspian looked at the crater that had been formed. More specifically, he looked at the creature who had formed the crater.

It stepped out of the crater with long strides. Large feet were covered in plated armor stained with rust. A chestplate that must have once gleamed brightly in the sunlight now clanked dully as it walked, disgusting and grimy, as though it had been covered in several centuries worth of blood. Spiked pauldrons sat on its shoulders, clinking together against the chestplate. A rusted steel helmet covered much of its face; everything save for the blood red eyes gazing out from within. Grasped firmly in its left hand was a massive claymore.

"Is that an undead?" Caspian asked. It didn't look like any undead he had ever seen or heard of before. It was too big. What was this thing?

A strange mist blew from its mouth, and a shriek not unlike the dying screams of a vengeful spirit accompanied it. The red eyes behind its helmet glowed with an ethereal malevolence. Whatever this thing was, it wasn't a regular undead.

It looked at Caspian. Then it switched its gaze to Elincia. Intelligence shone in its bloody eyes.

It roared, a noise that split the air, a sound that shook Caspian to his core and caused Elincia to stumble backwards. With one test swing of its claymore, the creature bent its knees and rushed forward faster than Caspian would have imagined possible for such a bulky creature.

The monster tried to close the distance between it and Elincia, but Caspian moved to intercept it. He raised his blade to block the creature's swing. Caspian only had a moment to realize his mistake before their blades made contact, and he was sent flying.

"Caspian!" Elincia screamed.

Twisting his body around, Caspian struck the ground feet first, kicking up dust and rocks as he skidded along the cobblestone road. Coming to a halt, he fell onto a knee and almost dropped his sword as agony lanced up his hands, arms, and shoulders.

It felt like his entire body had been shaken up. No, it felt like his body was shaking apart at the seams. The strength behind that single swing had been unlike anything he'd ever blocked. Even Derek would not have been able to produce that much power.

There's no way this is an undead. It's too powerful. Could this be the lich king?

Whatever this thing was, it was going after Elincia. Even though he was in pain, even though his limbs were shaking and his body ached, Caspian launched himself into an all-out sprint. He closed the distance between himself and this strange monster quickly. There was no way he could let it get near Elincia.

His first attack was blocked. He swung his blade downward as though to split this creature's head in half. The monster raised its massive claymore to intercept his attack, but Caspian didn't let that deter him, and he used the momentum generated from his previous attack to spin around and attack from a different angle.

"Halka—"

Caspian was ready to slice the claymore in half, depriving this monster of its weapon, but he would never get the chance. The creature stomped its foot on the ground before Caspian finished speaking. Without warning, the ground around them cracked and split open. Fissures spread from the underneath the monster's foot, traveling across the ground and causing the earth beneath Caspian's feet to shift.

Unable to maintain his balance, Caspian stumbled back. He was wide open, vulnerable, and the creature knew this, too. It raised its claymore high above its head, and then brought it down so quickly that the air howled.

There was no way Caspian would let himself get hit with that. He didn't bother trying to regain his balance. Instead he fell backwards, ignoring the jabbing pain as his back hit the ground, rolling across the street, and then coming back up on his feet.

The claymore struck the ground, barely missing Caspian, who could've sworn several epidermal layers of skin had been cut off his forehead. As the claymore sank into the earth, Caspian decided that now was his chance. He leapt forward and thrust his sword at the creature's chest.

"Halkaista!"

His sword went straight through the armor, piercing it and the creature's chest with ease. It sank in all the way to the hilt. Teeth grit, Caspian prepared to cut this creature apart.

He couldn't.

His hands wouldn't move.

Because they were trapped in an ironclad grip.

Caspian screamed as the hands, clad in bony iron plates, crushed his wrists. The heart-rending agony of his bones being ground into a fine powder was unbearable. Unable to maintain his grip on his sword, Caspian was forced to let go, and then he was forced to his knees. He struggled to get up, but not only was the pain overriding his ability to move, the monster before him was simply too strong.

Screaming reached him. High pitched. Female. Elincia. She was screaming at him, or was she screaming at the monster crushing his wrists? He couldn't tell.

I...

His wrists were suddenly released, though they were in so much pain he couldn't move them. It didn't matter anyway. A large hand grabbed his face seconds later. Caspian's scream was muffled as the hand clenched around his face. He screamed and screamed. But no matter how he screamed, kicked, and thrashed, nothing changed. His face felt like it was being squashed like a grape!

Am I going to die here?

Caspian thought he could see his life flashing before his eyes— or he would have, except the pain was so overwhelming that he couldn't see anything. All he saw was white. Nothing existed beyond the searing white that burned his vision.

It was just then, as his vision was beginning to turn black, that a voice called out.

"Odin! Help me, please!"

Something struck Caspian, a fierce gale that battered his already beaten body. The hand that had been gripping him, crushing his skull, released him, and he was sent flying backwards. He landed on the ground some distance away. His vision was blurry. He blinked several times, trying to clear it, and when his eyesight finally sharpened again, he saw something unbelievable.

The creature, towering above everyone, imposing beyond belief, was reeling backwards, an ear-splitting shriek resounding from within its helmet-clad head.

It wasn't the kind of scream he would've expected to hear from such a monster. It wasn't the ferocious roar of an undead abomination. It was a shrill cry, a scream of pain, an inhuman, incomprehensible noise that made Caspian wish he could cover his ears.

The creature was missing a hand.

The wound was clean. There was no blood. However, the hand that had been gripping him was no longer there. A stump now existed where the appendage had once been. Steam wafted from it as though it were a bonfire that had just been doused with water.

Impaled into the ground in front of the undead monster was a spear. Glimmering gold, the shaft was a lot longer than most normal spears. A network of glowing archaic runes were engraved upon its surface. While one side ended in a pointed pommel, the other end was unlike anything he had ever seen. A crescent blade extended from it. They looked like wings, almost, with two sharpened points in the front and back. After the crescent blade came the spear point.

Jagged and covered in spikes on either side, the spear ended in a sharp tip that looked like it could easily pierce through anything.

What is that?

That spear wasn't natural.

As a half-elf, Caspian was sensitive to the flows of magic and nature. He could sense the two, even if his abilities were nowhere near the same sensitivity of a pureblood elf.

The weapon before him, impaled into the ground as though it had been tossed there from the heavens, exuded an aura of might so immense that Caspian was shuddering just from being in close proximity to it. What's more…

This spear isn't natural.

It wasn't that the spear was unnatural, but that it didn't belong in this realm. It was not a spear meant for mortals to wield. That brought him to one conclusion.

It's a spirit's weapon.

There was still so much that no one knew about spirits. However, thanks to Elincia, Caspian could proudly state that he knew more than others. Spirits were generally anthropomorphic and had a purely human appearance—or perhaps it was the other way around? Either way, there were only a few spirits that didn't look human, such as the wolf spirit Fenrir, or the great serpent Jörmungandr.

Many of those spirits wielded powerful weapons. Freya's spear, for example. Every time Elincia summoned Freya, the power that came from her spear made the hairs on his neck tingle.

The spear before him was the same; it gave the same feeling, but even more immense, even more powerful.

"Caspian!" Elincia shouted. "Use Gungir to defeat that thing!"

Gungir?

Caspian stared at the weapon—even as the undead creature on the other side of it continued to scream as its stump of a wrist burned. Was that this weapon's name? He had never heard of a weapon being given a name, but perhaps spirits liked to name their weapons. Caspian didn't know if he could even wield such a weapon. His body, his arms in particular, were already crushed.

If only I had a spell that could strengthen my body...

The moment these thoughts passed through his mind; another miracle occurred.

Spellcasting was one of the three branches of elven magic. Unlike alchemists and nature manipulators, few could become a spellcaster if they didn't have the natural aptitude for it. In other words, if the spells weren't already engraved upon their souls, becoming a spellcaster was nearly impossible.

It was a magic that an elf had to be born with.

Buried deep within a spellcaster's soul, engraved upon their heart and born from scars of past traumas, were a number of words that invoked powers. Spells. These spells each conceived a different ability. The words used were different for everyone. Even if a spell used by one person invoked the same power, the spell used was different. Furthermore, the number of spells that a spellcaster could use was determined by the number of emotional scars that a person carried.

Caspian had three spells. Each one had been created due to a traumatic experience in his past. The ability to cut through every substance known to man. Halkaista. The ability to leap dozens of meters through the air. Springen. The power to reflect magical attacks back at their user. Cintittu.

They were abilities that had been created by his scars, his weaknesses, his self-loathing. Halkaista, a power born from the fear of being betrayed by someone he trusted. Springen, created by his desire to escape from the clutches of a world that refused to acknowledge him. Cintittu, a repulsive force that reflected and pushed away magic in the same way others had pushed him away. They were symbols of his weaknesses made manifest. It was part of the reason he had originally loathed using them.

And now, a new spell became engraved onto his soul. Vahvistaa. The ability to temporarily fortify and strengthen the body.

"V-Vahvistaa…"

A low groan escaped him as Caspian felt his mana circulating through his body. His bones snapped back into place with a painful hiss. Strength returned to him, though it came at the cost of incredible anguish. Even so, with this, he could move. He could act. He could fight.

Caspian stood up and grabbed the spear. He bit back a scream. The spear, it was burning him!

Smoke wafted from his hands as the spear, Gungnir, burned him. It wasn't just his body that was suffering. It felt like his very soul was being charbroiled, as if the spear, knowing that he was not its master, was attacking him.

He withstood the pain, pulled his lips back into a snarl, and yanked the spear from the ground. Gungnir was a heavy weapon. Caspian arms were almost yanked from their sockets as he first held it, even though he was being enhanced by magic. He imagined it was only thanks to his new spell that he could even carry this weapon.

With the knowledge that he would not be able to hold it for much longer, Caspian acted quickly, rushing straight at the undead monster, which had yet to notice him. It seemed this spear did more than just physical damage. The undead was still howling, still gripping its stump. Perhaps the continued pain the undead felt was due to Gungnir being a spirit weapon. It didn't matter. With a fierce shout, Caspian put all of the strength he had into his arms and jabbed the spear into the undead's chest.

"GGGGGRRRRAAAAAA!!!"

The shriek that rattled Caspian's bones sounded nothing like a human being. The undead, its chest pierced by Gungnir, wailed as it grabbed at the spear, only for the wailing to grow louder when the spear burned its only remaining hand. Steam rose from its hands and chest, becoming a plume that clogged the air.

Being so close, Caspian became a first-hand witness to the power this spear held as, like someone having all of the water sucked out of their body, the undead shriveled up. Bones cracked as the armor became too heavy. The undead's arms fell off, breaking apart like brittle twigs. Its legs snapped, crackling and popping as they disintegrated. Before too long, even its body became nothing but dust, until only the armor, still impaled by Gungnir, remained.

Caspian dropped the spear. It hit the ground with a hard crack, denting the road, and then it dispersed, bursting into particles of light that vanished seconds later.

It took him a moment to realize it, but with the undead creature gone, there were no more undead in the area. What was going on? He looked around before finally noticing it: The undead were all retreating. They moved back up the streets, leaving the mountain he, Elincia, and Catarina were defending. Did that mean they had won?

As the knowledge took place in his mind, Caspian felt his strength leave him. He sagged to the ground, exhausted, weary. He wanted to sleep. No, he wanted to cuddle up with Elincia and fall asleep in her arms.

Speaking of...

"Elincia!" Catarina's scream jolted Caspian out of his reverie.

He looked over at where the scream had come from. There, lying unconscious on the ground, with several people surrounding her, was Elincia.

Chapter 10

It was several hours after the battle. Caspian was tired. He longed for the feeling of a pillow under his head. However, he couldn't do that, not right now. The reason was because…

"I can't believe Elincia is an elf," Catarina said, shocked.

He and Catarina were in the bedroom that she had allowed him and Elincia to sleep in before the attack. Elincia was also there, but she was unconscious, her supine form lying on the bed. The covers were pulled up to her chest. The gentle swells of her breast rose and fell as she breathed deeply, and her eyes were closed, revealing thick, blonde lashes. Her cheeks were flushed and sweat covered her forehead.

Her ears were long and pointed.

During the battle, Elincia had used the last ounce of mana she possessed and had collapsed as result. Now she was unconscious, running a high fever from mana exhaustion, and the illusion that Loki had cast to hide her ears was gone.

Everyone in Flos had to know that she was an elf by now. Nearly half the population had seen her ears, and rumors tended to spread quickly.

"It was kept a secret from the general population since elves are so hated," Caspian said. While Catarina was sitting on a chair next to the bed, Caspian sat on the bed's edge. He tenderly stroked Elincia's hair and brushed back her bangs as she slept. "Elincia was rescued by Sylvia several years ago and came to live with her. According to what she told us, there was a revolt in Fas Sheras and she was forced to flee."

"I guess that explains why Lady Sylvia hasn't done anything about her." Catarina crossed her left leg over her right, hands on her kneecap as she stared at the blonde elf lying comatose on the bed. "But how did she become a sorceress? I thought elves couldn't summon spirits."

Caspian didn't say anything for a full minute. He continued to stroke Elincia's hair. Because she was unconscious, she wasn't dreaming, but he could still feel her through the bond, and he sent all of his feelings for her through it. Maybe it wouldn't help, but he liked to think that his feelings would reach her.

"Our knowledge of elves is extremely limited," Caspian said softly. "We don't really know if they're capable of summoning spirits or not. It might just be that none of them have ever tried, or maybe Elincia is special in some way. There's no way to know for sure without asking another elf directly."

"I guess so." Catarina stared at him, but he did his best to ignore her piercing expression. He stopped stroking Elincia's hair in exchange for cupping her cheek. She shifted against him, her face nuzzling his hand as if she could tell, unconsciously, that he was the one touching her. "You really love her, don't you?"

"Yes," he admitted. It was getting easier to say that the more often he said it. "I've loved her for a very long time now, ever since we were little."

"It must be nice having someone who is so special to you," Catarina said.

"Do you not have anyone who's special like that?" Caspian inquired.

Catarina shook her head. "When I was younger, I lived a very sheltered life. My parents would never let me go out, and I was very frail, so I got sick a lot. After they died, I didn't have any time to concern myself with matters of love. I needed to learn how to be a proper leader and set an example for my people."

"I'm sorry."

"I don't see why you would be." Shrugging, Catarina leaned back in her chair and looked at the ceiling. A small smile played on her lips. "I've never been too interested in romance anyway. To me, making sure my people are happy and healthy is more important than whether I have a man by my side or not."

While he didn't say anything, Caspian was impressed by Catarina's dedication toward her people. It seemed that she, unlike most nobles, was actually concerned about whether or not the people she was in charge of were cared for. That was rare. Most nobles were scum, and while Catarina could have been lying to him, the fact that she had fought by his side for her people lent credence to her words.

"How do you feel about Elincia now that you know what she is?" Caspian asked. "Are you frightened of her now that you know she's an elf? Do you hate her?"

If Catarina disliked Elincia, then his estimation of her would drop.

To his great relief, Catarina shook her head. "After what she's done for my people, I don't see how I could possibly hate her for being an elf. There's no point in hating someone because they were born differently. Besides, it's been a long time since humans have fought with elves."

It was probably the first time anyone had said this. Sure, there were a few people in Casadinia who had not treated Elincia differently after they learned that she was an elf, but only a handful had ever outright said that it didn't matter. That made her words hold a lot more meaning.

She could have been lying, but for once, he decided to believe in someone.

"Thank you," Caspian said quietly.

Catarina smiled as she stood up. "I'm going to bed. You should get some sleep as well. All three of us have had a long day."

As Catarina left, Caspian turned back to Elincia and continued to idly stroke her hair.

Wake up soon, he sent these thoughts through the bond.

He didn't receive an answer.

Naturally.

***

Elincia woke up some time the next morning, but she was still so exhausted that she could hardly move at all. It took an entire day for Elincia to recover from her mana exhaustion. During that time, Caspian did what he could to care for her, propping her pillow, wiping the sweat from her forehead, and making sure she had no need for anything. It would have not been inaccurate to say he had acted like her nanny.

He also helped Catarina and her people burn their dead. The mother of the young girl that he had rescued turned out to be one of those who had been killed, so Catarina decided to adopt her.

Not surprisingly, the girl had bawled at the funeral. She didn't even seem to understand, but she had still cried her eyes out, perhaps knowing instinctively that she would never see her mother again.

Funerals held like this did not mean burying the dead since they'd been bitten by undead, which could cause them to turn if left alone. Normally, a sorceress would have been responsible for sanctifying the remains, but this town had no sorceress, so they simply created a funeral pyre and cremated the bodies.

After Elincia recovered, she and Catarina spoke many times, debating on what they should do to prevent an attack like this from happening again.

Elincia believed that abandoning Flos and traveling to a village further west was the best idea. Catarina disagreed. She did not want to leave her home, even if that meant weathering another undead

147

attack. Caspian had been witness to their dispute.

"I know it might seem hard to leave your home," Elincia said as she sat in the bed, the blanket covering her legs. She didn't bother casting the illusion over her ears anymore since everyone already knew she was an elf. Her long ears wiggled from as she continued speaking. "But I really think leaving this city and traveling further west would be better for you and your people. Caspian and I must continue moving to discover how far the lich king's influence has spread, so we can't remain here to protect you. If the undead came back…"

"I understand what you are saying, but Flos is my home. I can't abandon it," Catarina said as she sat beside the bed.

"It isn't like I don't understand how you feel, but…"

"Look. I understand your concern, but I'm sorry. I just can't leave Flos. I can't."

Catarina was stubborn about remaining in Flos no matter what happened, to the point where she stubborn refused to leave no matter what. In the end, they had created a compromise: guards would be posted along the borders of Flos, and should they spot undead coming in their direction, they would alert Catarina and begin the evacuation to the nearest city. Elincia had still not approved, but she knew it was the best possible compromise.

On a more pleasant note, the people of Flos had not discriminated against Elincia after she woke up. When she and Caspian walked through the city, many people had thanked her for saving them. Some of the children had even presented her with flowers.

Elincia had been so surprised that she had actually burst into tears. Caspian could still remember how the many people who had crowded around her, thanking her for protecting them, had panicked when she began bawling like a child. Just remembering what happened brought a smile to his face.

They spent two more days in Flos. While the city hadn't received much damage, there were many people who had been injured, and Elincia, being the kind of woman who couldn't leave when people were in need, spent the first of those two days summoning Eir to heal everyone.

Consequently, the second day had been spent with her bedridden because she had exhausted her mana supply. Again.

On the third morning of the third day, Caspian and Elincia were standing outside of the city borders. They weren't alone. Catarina and many of the citizens had come to see them off.

"I suppose it would be a bad idea to ask if you could stay," Catarina said.

Elincia smiled. "Yes. We can't afford to stay here. There's no telling how far the lich king's influence has spread in other directions, so we need to find that out."

"Yeah, I figured that would be the case." With a weary sigh, Catarina rubbed the back of her head, and then, throwing caution to the wind, pulled a surprised Elincia into a hug. "Try not to be a stranger. We'd love it if you came to visit us sometime in the future."

Elincia, after recovering from her shock, hugged the woman back. "I will. I promise."

Several kids ran up to Elincia and tugged at her dress. All of them were around ages from five to ten. The oldest one, a boy with brown hair and eyes, gave her a look that Caspian didn't really appreciate but couldn't do anything about. He hoped the boy's mother would paddle his bottom while giving him a lecture about not ogling someone who was clearly in a relationship.

Damn brat.

"Promise you'll come back and see us, Big Sister!" they all said at the same time.

Elincia blushed and smiled, and Caspian thought he saw some tears in her eyes, though none fell. She reached out, ruffling their heads.

"Of course I'll come visit."

"Yay!"

Just then, the ten-year-old decided to be bold. He hugged Elincia and buried his face in her chest. She seemed surprised, but after a moment, she merely smiled and patted the boy's head, completely oblivious to how that damn brat was burying his face in her bosoms.

Caspian scowled. What he wouldn't give to rip that little boy a new asshole—

"Be sure to protect Elincia, all right?" Catarina said.

The scowl on his face grew. "You don't have to tell me that. I'll gladly lay down my life for her."

"That's what I like to hear." Catarina grinned at him before turning to Elincia, who no longer had a boy buried face first in her chest, thank the spirits. "And you, make sure this guy doesn't do anything too reckless."

"Oi!" Caspian said, annoyed.

"I'll do my best," Elincia answered. "But I don't believe that's possible."

"Oi!" Caspian said again and was ignored.

More goodbyes were given, with many of the well-wishers calling out to Elincia, asking/demanding that she come back to visit and that they were welcome any time. Eventually, the time to finally leave drew upon them. Before they could go, as in, just as they had turned around and began to walk off, Catarina called out to them.

"By the way, Elincia!" When both he and Elincia turned around, Catarina gave them the widest grin she could muster, a literal ear to ear grin that split her face in half. "I like you better with pointy ears! You should keep them like that!"

Elincia touched her ears. Since everyone already knew she was an elf, she hadn't bothered asking Loki to cast an illusion on her. Thus her long ears with their pointy tips were on full display. Caspian didn't say anything because he had already told her much the same already, but he agreed with Catarina.

Smiling widely, Elincia gave everyone one last wave before she and Caspian set off again. They walked down the dirt road, listening to the people calling out to them. Caspian turned his head one last time. Catarina and the others were no more than specks now, and half an hour after they began walking, they could no longer be seen.

"Where are we going to next?" asked Elincia as the village of

Flos slowly disappeared into the distance.

"If we follow the map, then our next destination is going to be Calidum Vere," Caspian said.

"Isn't that a hot spring village?" asked Elincia.

"It is," Caspian confirmed. "They're well known for being only one of six natural hot springs in Arcadia."

Hot springs were rare in Arcadia… well, naturally built ones. It had something to do with the geography. Arcadia had no active volcanoes, nor did it have any thermal heating vents, which were what hot springs came from. Caspian didn't understand much more than that.

"I love hot springs!" Elincia said… then paused. "Well, I've actually never been to a real hot spring before, but I've always wanted to visit one."

"Provided it's not overrun with undead, we might be able to take a short break." Caspian shrugged. "But I somehow don't think we're going to be that lucky."

Elincia's shoulders drooped. "Way to kill my mood."

"… Sorry."

"You're not sorry at all."

Interlude 11

Sylvia sat under the shade of a gazebo, in a garden filled with lilacs, daffodils, and various other flowers. Sitting before her on a marble table was a soothing cup of chamomile tea.

It was one of her rare breaks. While many of her fellow sorceresses often called her a workaholic, even she needed to rest every once in a while. During these times when a break was necessary, she would often come out to the flower gardens and relax under the shade, enjoying the refreshing scent from the many different types of flora.

"My Lady?"

Her hand twitched. D'artagnan rarely spoke unless spoken to. That he was calling out to her meant he had something important to say.

"Yes?"

"May I ask… why you decided to send Caspian and Elincia to Parumé. I know that you wanted to get them out of Casadinia, but would it not have been better to give them a task that was less dangerous?"

Odd...

D'artagnan was not one for nonsensical questions, but Sylvia could not determine the purpose of this one. Was he concerned about Caspian? She supposed that, as a fellow knight, it was an appropriate response, something to do with camaraderie, perchance?

Sylvia could not see D'Artagnan's face because he was not sitting with her. He stood outside of the gazebo, keeping watch on their surroundings. That was his way. He never allowed himself to rest when they were together, even when she was not working herself. It was the way a sorceress's knight should behave.

Caspian could stand to learn from D'Artagnan's example.

"Perhaps it would have been safer to give them another task." Sylvia took a sip of her tea, sighed as the herbal effects soothed her nerves, set it back down, and continued. "As of this moment, Caspian and Elincia are powerful but untested. What's more, Caspian has many emotional scars that he never let heal." She paused, recalling the memories that had receded into her mind with time. "Ever since I rescued Caspian from Parumé, he has done his best to forget about that time. His memories are buried so deeply within him that the only memory remaining is the one memory he can never forget."

"The day Parumé was destroyed by undead?" D'artagnan guessed.

"Correct." Tracing a finger along the lip of her teacup, Sylvia brought up more memories of the young man that she had rescued years ago. "That memory is so powerful that it's been ingrained into his psyche. However, all of the other memories he has are being suppressed."

"And you are hoping that by sending him back to Parumé, he will be forced to confront his past," D'artagnan deduced.

The sound of a songbird made Sylvia look up. Two birds were fluttering overhead, dancing around each other in what she guessed was some form of mating ritual. It wasn't long before the birds set down on the roof and snuggled together.

She frowned at the birds before dismissing them in favor of answering D'artagnan.

"It is just as you say. Caspian is not like you. He is controlled by his emotions, and when they become too much, he runs away from them. I'm hoping that by sending him on this mission, he can overcome what happened in his past and grow stronger. If he can do that, then perhaps he can learn to overcome his other emotional hang ups."

Caspian didn't know it, but Sylvia had kept an eye on him during his time at the academy. At her behest, Headmaster Stratello had sent her bi-annual reports on Caspian's progress. She knew everything that had happened to him. The bullying, the isolation, the hatred. Sylvia had not intervened since part of Arcadia's Knight Academy's policies forbade sorceresses from interfering with the students' growth—she had already interfered enough just by letting him attend—and she had also hoped he would become stronger.

Instead he had crawled further into a shell. He had created a shield. When someone picked a fight, he responded with violence. When someone insulted him, he insulted right back. Caspian had become the very thing he hated without even realizing it.

Not even teachers were spared from his actions. Sylvia didn't know if she could blame Caspian—she remembered how he had almost been killed by a noble who befriended him and then stabbed him in the back—but she had hoped that he would overcome his issues without aid. That he had not done so was disappointing.

"Are you sure it's wise to force this confrontation?" D'artagnan asked. "What if he's not ready?"

"Have you so little faith in the boy?" Sylvia answered him with a question of her own. "While he didn't progress much at the academy, Caspian has made many strides since graduating. His mentality, strength, and rationality have improved. I trust that he can overcome this obstacle."

She looked down at the still warm tea. Steam rose from the cup.

She took another sip.

She set the cup back down.

"He'll need to if he wants to overcome the hardships that are likely to befall him and Elincia in the future," she finished. To that, D'artagnan said nothing.

The two songbirds sitting on the roof flapped their wings and took off, flying to parts unknown.

Afterword

Hello all. Welcome to the next volume of my light novel series, Arcadia's Ignoble Knight: The Lich King Part I. As the name implies, this volume is about a lich king.

Maybe.

I think I mentioned it previously, but this arc is going to be much darker than my previous arcs. I plan on going into Caspian's past, digging up some very unpleasant memories, and forcing him to confront things he tried to forget.

I'm just nice like that.

This volume was a little short. The Lich King is split up into two parts because of how long this arc is. I promise, the next part will be much longer, meatier, and juicier. You'll be able to sink your teeth into it!

In any case, I hope you all enjoyed this volume. If you did, consider leaving a review. Reviews are the lifeblood of an author. They are not only vital for our continued success but positive and constructive reviews can help us grow.

A few last minute thanks before I head off. I would first like to thank my editor and proofreaders. My story would be trash without them.

I would also like to thank Claparo for coming with me this far into the series. He does some great artwork and is probably one of my favorite artists.

Lastly, I would like to thank you readers. None of this would be possible without you. I'm incredibly thankful for your continued support. I hope I can continue relying on your support in the days to come as I continue my writing journey.

~Brandon Varnell

Did you know that I'm creating an American Kitsune manga?! Production will begin sometime in 2020 on Patreon. Here is a sneak peak!

If you would like to support the creation of American Kitsune the manga, please head to https://www.patreon.com/BrandonVarnell and subscribe today!

HAVE YOU EVER EXPERIENCED ONE OF THOSE LIFE-CHANGING INSTANCES? AN EVENT SO MOMENTOUS THAT, YEARS LATER, YOU'RE STILL MARVELING AT HOW IT CHANGED YOUR LIFE?
I HAD ONE OF THOSE. IT HAPPENED A WHILE AGO
EVEN TO THIS DAY, THROUGH ALL THE CHANGES THAT HAVE HAPPENED, THROUGH ALL THE EXPERIENCES THAT I'VE BEEN THROUGH, I STILL CAN'T BELIEVE HOW THIS ONE MOMENT CHANGED MY LIFE FOREVER.
NO MATTER WHAT CAME AFTER, OUR FIRST MEETING IS SOMETHING THAT I'LL ALWAYS REMEMBER.

ESPECIALLY SINCE, AT THE BEGINNING OF THIS TALE, I THOUGHT SHE WAS NOTHING BUT AN ORDINARY FOX WITH, UNORDINARILY ENOUGH, TWO BUSHY RED TAILS.

LIFE

IT HITS YOU WHEN YOU LEAST EXPECT IT TO.

AMERICAN
KITSUNE

Arcadia's IgnobleKnight
Volumes 1-6
are available now!

Volumes 1-6 are available now!
A Most Unlikely Hero

American Kitsune
volumes 1-11
are available now!

The Executioner Series
The complete series
is available now!

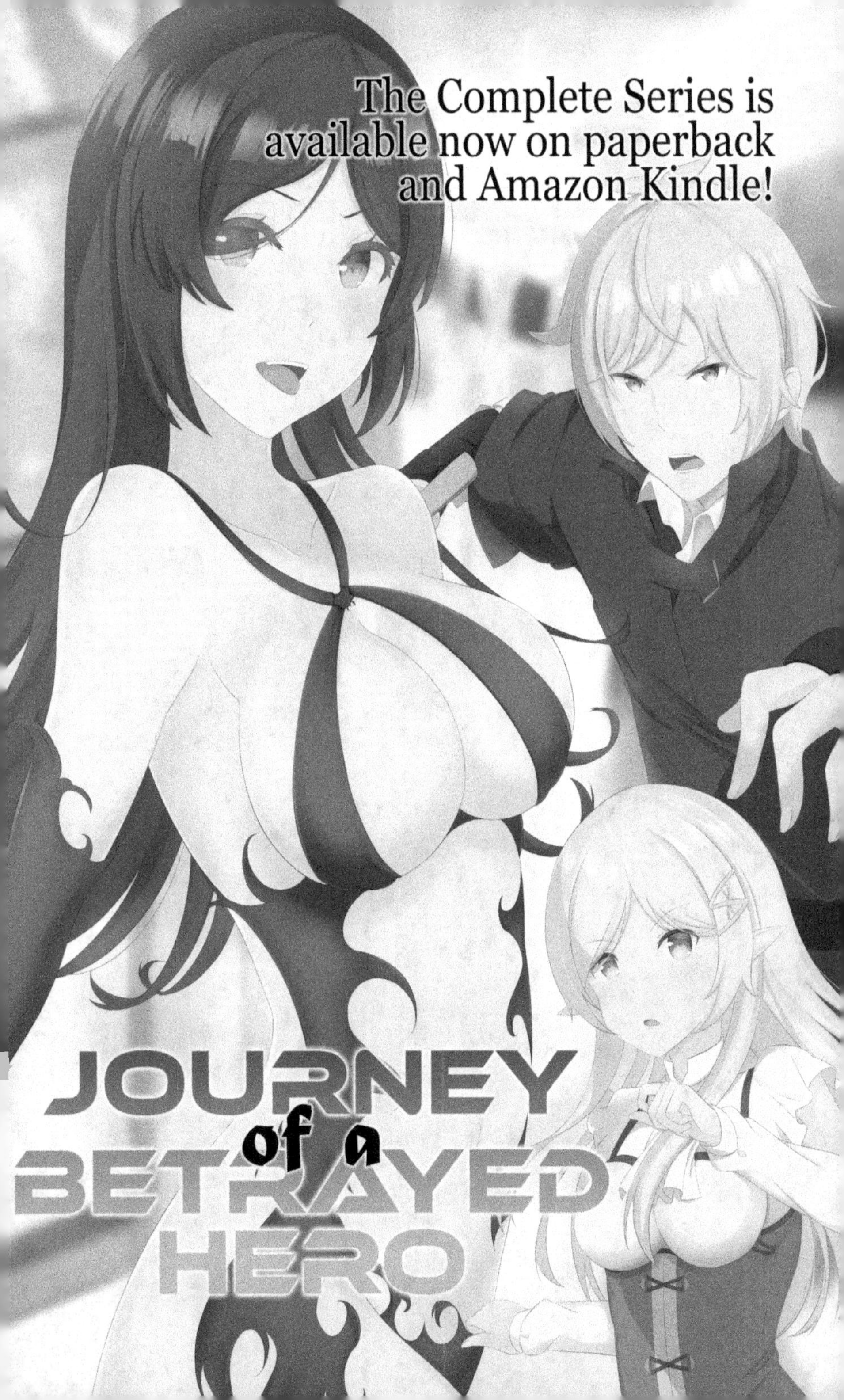
The Complete Series is available now on paperback and Amazon Kindle!
JOURNEY of a BETRAYED HERO

WIEDERGEBURT 1
LEGEND OF THE REINCARNATED WARRIOR
Volume 1 & 2
are available on Pre Order!

RIFT WARS: ORIGINS
Volume 1 Available now!
Swordsman Of the Rift
Author
Brandon Varnell
Artist
Lonwa A